HIS AUTUMN NEIGHBOR

HOME TO ORCHARD SPRINGS

LEE TOBIN MCCLAIN

GRACE PORTER BOOKS

PLUS A BONUS NOVELLA

PRAISE FOR LEE TOBIN MCCLAIN

"Lee Tobin McClain dazzles with unforgettable characters, fabulous small-town settings and a big dose of heart."

—Susan Mallery, New York Times bestselling author

"Lee Tobin McClain's books make my heart sing."

—Debbie Macomber, New York Times bestselling author

"[A] magnetic second chance romance... McClain pits her charming, authentic characters against the realistic problems of everyday life, making for a story that is deeply emotional but never soapy...Readers won't want to put this down."

—Publishers Weekly, STARRED REVIEW of *The Forever Farmhouse*

1

Will Burton looked around his new home, golden with September sunshine. His shoulders relaxed as he drank in the quiet and solitude.

The small Pennsylvania farmhouse had belonged to his grandparents and held fond memories for him. It also held the possibility of getting what he wanted and needed most: peace.

The red gingham curtains and embroidered samplers on the walls were his grandmother's style, a little frou-frou for a thirty-something combat veteran. Same with the knitted blankets folded atop the big, overstuffed couch and the frilly throw pillows at either end. His buddies would laugh, but Will didn't care. The only modernization he planned on was replacing the rabbit-ear TV with a big new flatscreen.

The place was compact for a farmhouse: kitchen, living room, and dining room on this floor, two bedrooms upstairs. Front porch complete with rocking chairs, where he intended to spend some very pleasant and peaceful evenings.

A knock on the back door startled him. He hadn't expected company way out on this rural road. There was only one other farm out this way, Abbott Farm. The rest of the road was lined with cornfields and trees.

He opened the back door and was surprised to see Stone Smith, one of the Abbott Farm crowd. He and Stone had hung out together during Will's summer visits as a teenager, had chased girls together, done some partying. They'd gotten reacquainted a couple years ago in the farm country outside Nashville.

Will liked Stone, but... so much for solitude. He forced a welcoming smile onto his face. "Come on in. I was just about to make coffee." He shook the man's hand and then rummaged through his kitchen cupboards. "Still figuring out where I put everything. Go ahead, have a seat."

He wondered what Stone wanted but didn't ask. Small talk first—that was the country way.

He found a box of coffee pods and popped one into the machine. "Heard you got married," he said to Stone. "Congratulations, man." He clapped Stone on the back as he walked to the refrigerator to find the milk.

"Thanks. Elena is the best. And Maddie, our daughter, is amazing. Wait till you meet her."

Stone had never mentioned having a kid. Maybe he just meant that he was a stepdad to his wife's child.

The thing was, Will really didn't want to meet Stone's daughter, nor anyone else for that matter. He wanted to be alone.

He put a cup of coffee in front of Stone, along with a carton of milk, and fixed himself a cup, too.

Stone thanked him. "Heard you're here to stay," he said. "Still restoring vintage farm equipment?" When they'd reconnected outside Nashville, Stone had sent some business Will's way.

"Uh-huh. When my grandparents decided to move to Florida, they asked if I wanted to take over this place, and I jumped on it. The barn's perfect for my work."

"Makes sense. House is solid, too." Stone cleared his throat. "I wanted to talk about your tenant," he said.

"Tenant?" Will drew a blank.

"Out there." Stone gestured toward the open screen door. A shed-like structure was visible past the porch.

"Oh, yeah. Grandma said someone was moving in." That had been a project of Grandpa's, remaking an old shed into one of those tiny houses. There had been some thought of renting it out as an Airbnb, but then his grandparents had gotten tired of the cold weather in Pennsylvania. They'd left without getting into the vacation-stay business.

"It's my sister who's renting it out," Stone said. "My foster sister, I mean. Allie."

"Oh. I didn't know." Will remembered Allie as a cute girl, her dark hair in pigtails, always running around with another foster sister about the same age. Both were part of the so-called Flock: four foster kids who'd lived at Abbott Farm as teenagers and stayed close as adults.

"Yeah," Stone said. "She's been a kindergarten teacher for a few years out of state. Now she's moved back. She's setting up a program at the farm for grade school kids to come and visit on field trips."

"Nice." Will tried to sound more sincere than he felt. He hoped any children who visited would stay on Abbott Farm. He didn't need a bunch of noisy kids around here.

The thought of kids brought a memory flash of a dark-haired Middle Eastern child. His stomach clenched and he stared at his coffee, taking deep breaths.

Don't go there. Don't.

"Did you hear me?" Stone's voice was overly loud, as if he'd asked the question more than once.

Will brought himself back into the present moment. Grandma's kitchen. Neighbor across the table from him. "Sorry, man," he said. "What did you say?"

"I said, stay away from her."

"What?" Will looked at Stone's serious, frowning face, confused.

"She's not your kind of girl," Stone said. "You need to keep your distance."

Fractured bits of flashbacks lingered. Will kept up the deep breathing, trying to pick up the thread of the conversation. Oh yeah. Allie, Stone's foster sister. "What are we talking about here?"

"I mean, she'd not an option for you to... date."

Understanding hit him. "Oh! No, no way. I'm not like that anymore."

"Right." Stone looked skeptical.

"Really. I've changed." Will vaguely remembered his girl-chasing, heartbreaking stage. But since his stint overseas, he wasn't that person anymore. "I've gotten pretty solitary," he said. "I'm focused on my work. Don't need, or want, too much contact with people. Especially women."

"Uh-huh." Stone clearly didn't believe him.

"I'm just looking for peace. Doing my work, reminding folks about the old times." It was work that helped people rather than hurting them.

"I'll be close by," Stone said.

Will raised an eyebrow. "If that's a warning, it's not necessary."

Stone studied him as if trying to read his mind, his sincerity. Finally, he spoke again. "Maybe you *have* changed."

"I have. You've got nothing to worry about."

"I'll be running the farm operations over at Abbott, turning it organic," Stone told him. "If you remember my foster brother, David, he and his wife are in charge of the farm stand. Our sister Jenn's got a flower business going. She married Eddie Wilson. Remember him? So anyway, we'll all be around."

Will was amused. The point seemed to be that Stone's sister Allie had plenty of protectors just down the road.

Fine with him. All the action at Abbott Farm should keep the woman busy and out of his hair.

Stone drank the rest of his coffee. He stood. "Good talking, man," he said. "I actually have an old hand plow I'd like restored in time for Christmas. A surprise for Pop Abbott. You got room in your schedule?"

"Absolutely. Bring it on over anytime."

Stone headed for the door, then turned. "We're having a Labor Day cookout, and you're welcome to join in. Monday, dinnertime."

"Thanks. I might."

After Stone left, Will closed the door and frowned. He probably ought to go to the cookout, make nice with his neighbors. Reassure them he wasn't any kind of threat.

But socializing with the Abbott Farm crew would be a one-time event. He didn't want his busy-sounding neighbors to detract from the peace he was looking for.

2

It was so, so good to be home.

Allie Walker cleared the last of the plates from the long picnic table at Abbott Farm and headed into the farmhouse. They'd had a lovely Labor Day cookout, partly in honor of her finally moving back to the area, which was sweet. Mostly family, a few friends, and people who worked the farm.

Allie's foster sister and best friend, Jenn, came up beside her, a tray of dirty utensils in her hands. "Thanks for doing that," Jenn said. "You don't have to clean up."

"Yes, I do. This is home, and I'm family."

Allie set down her stack of plates and started running water into the old-fashioned double sink.

As they started to wash—something they'd done together in this very spot many, many times in their teenage years—Jenn glanced over at her, then nodded out the window. "Did you talk to your new neighbor?"

Allie looked out. There was Will Burton, who had moved onto the farm where her new tiny house was located. "Yeah," she said. "We said hello. He doesn't seem very friendly." She'd recognized Will from years ago, when he was around visiting his grandparents. You couldn't help noticing him, with his muscular good looks. He was a friend of Stone's, but he was ten years older than her, at least, so she didn't know him well.

Jenn dunked a couple of serving plates into soapy dishwater. "According to Stone, he can be *too* friendly."

Allie raised an eyebrow. "Not to me, apparently. Which is fine." She rinsed the plates Jenn handed her and started wiping the counter.

"Good. Will is too old and cranky for you,

but I *am* hoping you'll meet some nice guys now that you've moved back."

"Nope," Allie said. "I'm here to build a rewarding professional life, not to get burned again. I don't need to have another man dump me."

"All men aren't like that," Jenn said, frowning. "Although… I've heard rumors that Will tends to love 'em and leave 'em."

"Not my worry. I'm too busy for men. Allie scrubbed at Pop's old-fashioned stove. "I'm focused on prepping Abbott Farm for field trips. Plus I'm going to be out and about town, drumming up more business."

"Great," Jenn said. "For once, I'm more interested in the farm than in matchmaking, too. The more kids who come to your programs, the more parents know about the new Abbott Farm and all we have to offer."

Pop Abbott came inside and approached, putting an arm around each of them. He was more stooped than he'd been when Allie was a teen, but he still had the warm sparkle in his eyes. "This is a good sight, having you back in my kitchen."

"Oh, Pop." Allie leaned her head on his shoulder. "I'm so glad to be here."

It was true. Pop did seem to have recovered some after losing Ma Abbott, but he was alone in the world except for the four foster kids he'd helped raise, plus his own son, Ronald, who was not a great guy.

Pop Abbott had done so much for Allie when she was an abandoned mess of a young teenager. She owed him everything, and she meant to pay it back.

She dried her hands and hugged him. "I'm gonna drag you into giving talks to the school kids who come visit. I want you to tell them all about the life of a farmer."

Pop laughed. "You know I can talk. Just as long as I don't have to do any real work."

"We'll keep it minimal," Allie promised.

They finished their cleanup and then strolled outside and into the gathering twilight. There was a hint of fall in the air, and darkness was coming earlier these days. She wished she'd brought a sweater. It was getting chilly.

As they approached the rest of the group, Allie slowed down and spoke to Jenn and Pop. "As much as I'd like to stay, I'd better get home and attack that big stack of boxes in the tiny house. They're not going to unpack themselves."

"You need a ride back?" Jenn asked. "You walked over, didn't you?"

"Yes, and I'll walk back home. It's just half a mile."

Pop frowned. "It's getting a little dark," he said. He spotted Will and gestured to him. "You said you were headed out soon. Can you give Allie a ride?"

Will glanced at her. "No problem," he said. His voice indicated the exact opposite: it *was* a problem.

Grouchy guy. Allie shrugged it off. "That would be great, thanks." She turned away from him and hugged Jenn and Pop, and then Stone, who'd come over. She waved to David and Courtney, who were deep in conversation with one of their seasonal employees.

"Truck's over this way," Will said, jerking his head to the side.

Stone pinned Will with a level stare. "Remember what I told you."

Will gave a mock salute.

When they reached the vintage vehicle—one of those old-fashioned farm trucks that always showed up on Christmas cards—he opened the passenger door for her. So at least he had some manners. But once he climbed in and started driving, the only sound was the old engine's chugging.

"Thanks for doing this," Allie said, just to fill the silence. "What did Stone mean, remember what I told you?"

"That you're off limits."

"What? I'm gonna kill him." She frowned and added, "Although, it's true. I *am* off limits."

"Not a problem from my end," Will said.

Thanks a lot, she thought. That was typical of men. Or not completely typical. At least he wasn't pretending to like her, only to let her down later.

They drove the rest of the way in silence, and once they reached the property, she climbed out quickly. The sound of crickets rose up around her. The sky had turned lavender, and the moon was starting to rise. "Thanks," she said, slamming the door.

"No problem." Will turned away.

Allie started toward her tiny house, but a sound stopped her. A crying sound. It came from the direction of Will's farmhouse.

She stopped and looked back at Will. "What's that?"

"No clue," he said, frowning.

"It sounds like... a child," she said, and they both started jogging toward the farmhouse porch.

3

As they rushed toward the sound of the crying child, Will felt the flashbacks coming. Black hair, shining under a desert sun. Imad's normally sweet face, twisted with a darker emotion. The boy's mother's high-pitched words choked out in a language he barely understood. Brown eyes, full of tears and terror.

His face heated and his heart started to pound.

Later, he told himself. He could freak out later. This was an emergency. He had to deal with whatever was happening now.

As they reached the porch, the sound of deep, staccato woofs covered the child's cries.

He held out an arm, stopping Allie. "Careful. Wait."

Squinting through the twilight, he made out a squat black dog, weaving back and forth, growling and barking. A dachshund? How could that little dog be so loud?

And then he spotted a small boy behind the dog, his arms hugging his bent legs to his chest.

What in the world?

Will knelt and held his hand out toward the dog, but it gave a deep "grrr" and showed its teeth, so he pulled his hand back.

Allie sat down on the porch steps, opposite where the child was and several feet away, and spoke over the dog's barking. "Hi! Is this your dog? What's his name?"

"Gus," the little boy said. He pulled the dog into his lap. "Ssssh!"

The dog quieted a little. Now, at least, there were spaces between the barks.

Allie looked up at Will. "Do you know this kiddo?"

Will shook his head. "Never saw him before." He pulled out his phone, prepared to put in an emergency call.

The boy thrust something at Allie. Thin, white. An envelope.

Allie glanced at it. "Looks like a letter for you," she said, and passed it over to Will.

The envelope said "To Will Burton" on the outside.

Allie was still talking to the little boy, in a quiet, perky voice. She scooted a little closer, smiling, commenting on the dog. Will was briefly glad that she was here. A kindergarten teacher was a good ally in this bizarre situation.

"What's your name?" Allie was asking the child.

Will pulled the letter from the envelope and skimmed the first part. "Eli," he said. "Apparently his name is Eli, and he's five years old." He looked at the boy, who nodded and held up five fingers. In his lap, the dog had quieted down but remained watchful.

Will went back to the beginning of the page-long, handwritten letter, vaguely aware of Allie's soothing voice in the background. Then he read it again. His heart settled into a steady, hard pounding.

One line jumped out. He kept rereading it.

Eli is your son.

Will slid his phone back into his pocket without placing the emergency call. He stared at the little boy, feelings ricocheting through his head.

Five years old. This child, Eli, was the same age as Imad, the child who had died overseas. In Will's mind, Eli kept morphing into that other boy.

Will thought of Imad's mother, talking soothingly to him, just as Allie was doing.

He turned and walked a few steps away into the darkness, pressing his hands to his temples. Could it be? Was this possibly his child?

He studied the letter again, squinting, pulling it close to his face to decipher the messily handwritten words. He checked the bottom of the letter again. No signature.

The writer revealed that the child's medical records were in the backpack. That he should be entering kindergarten this fall. That he knew his letters and was smart.

At the end, she said she was the boy's mother and couldn't take care of him anymore.

That burned Will with indignation. Who did that?

And who *was* this woman? Who had he been with, five or six years ago?

Allie opened a plastic container she'd been holding this whole time. Leftovers from the cookout. She pulled something out and held it up to show the child. "Do you like brownies?"

"Yeah!" he said eagerly, reaching for it. The dog lifted his nose toward the brownie, too. Its tail started to wag.

"Your dog can't have any," Allie said. "It's not good for him."

"Okay." The little boy pushed the dog off his lap and grabbed the brownie. He stuffed it into his mouth.

Sympathy stirred in Will. The kid was hungry.

He kept reviewing the letter, trying to understand. "Do you see a backpack?" he asked Allie. This was surreal. He was amazed that his voice was coming out calm. He certainly didn't feel calm.

Still chewing, the boy pointed at a camo backpack, stuffed full.

Allie stood and took a few steps back to

stand beside Will. "What does the letter say? We should get him inside. Maybe call social services or the police."

"The letter says..." Will couldn't bring himself to speak it aloud. "Let's take him inside for the moment," he said. "The police would upset him. And if they take him away, he couldn't keep his dog."

"Good point." Allie took a few steps back toward the child, and the dog let out a couple of deep barks. "There's probably milk inside, to go with the brownies," she said to the boy, "and it's warmer. Do you want to come in?"

The boy stood up and grabbed his backpack. "Okay. Can I have another?"

She smiled at him. "We might be able to find you something healthier to eat first."

They walked inside, Allie still talking soothingly to the boy, and the dachshund sticking close to the boy's other side. Will brought up the rear and stopped just outside the door, his head spinning.

Could it be true?

He'd partied hard and had a lot of hookups that he regretted, back before everything had changed for him.

But he had always been careful to use protection, wanting to avoid this very situation. Was this a setup? Only Will wasn't a likely candidate to be taken advantage of. He wasn't wealthy or well known. Who would make up something like this?

Allie flipped on a light as she and Eli walked toward the kitchen. Still on the porch, Will studied the boy's lanky build and brown hair. Very much like childhood photos of himself.

A sick feeling rose in him. Maybe Eli *was* his child. He sucked in a few breaths of fresh, cool air before walking inside and shutting the door behind him.

He had the sense that, for better or worse, he was shutting the door on his old life and walking into a new one.

4

Allie stepped cautiously past the dachshund as it wove around her feet, panting, its eyes never leaving the child. She sat the child down at Will's kitchen table, wondering what on earth was going on. Why had Eli been left here?

She studied the little boy in the kitchen light, looking for signs of abuse or neglect. As a teacher, she was a mandated reporter, required by law to contact the authorities if she saw any suggestion of abuse or neglect.

But Eli's clothes were clean and his cheeks were full and healthy. True, he'd been crying, but he'd stopped and come inside with them willingly. Almost as if he knew them.

Contacting the authorities would make for a long, scary night for Eli. And as Will had pointed out, he'd have to be separated from the dog he obviously loved.

Will came into the kitchen, his expression suggesting that he was utterly at a loss, far more than Allie. He obviously wasn't going to be able to make a quick decision about what to do, even though this was his problem more than hers. Eli had been left on Will's front porch, with a letter addressed to Will.

Allie knelt beside Eli and held a hand out to the anxious little dog. "Do you think I can pet Gus?" she asked the boy.

He nodded and clicked his tongue at the dog, and it sniffed Allie's hand. Progress.

The kitchen was a cozy place with old-fashioned appliances and soft lighting. She looked at Will and nodded at the old-fashioned refrigerator. "If you have milk, pour him a glass, would you?"

Will walked immediately to the refrigerator, seeming relieved to have something to do.

She sat down catty-corner from the boy. "Were you out on the porch for a long time?" she asked.

He shook his head. "Not very long. Mommy's friend just left."

Allie wondered whether the friend had waited to see them coming. That would point to decent concern for young Eli.

Gus plopped down onto his side. Apparently, he'd decided his charge was safe enough that he could take a nap.

"Where is Mommy?" she asked the little boy.

He shook his head. "She's sick," he said. "She had to go away."

Allie blew out a breath and looked up at Will, who was setting a glass of milk in front of the child.

He looked as concerned and confused as she felt.

Eli took a big gulp of milk and wiped the back of his hand across his mouth. "Mommy said you were nice and would take care of me," he said, looking from Allie to Will and back again.

"Whoa," Will said.

"Whoa is right." Apparently, this wasn't

an accident or a random abandonment. And it didn't seem to be temporary, either. What on earth?

She felt as if she were watching a movie with an unbelievable plot. Leaving a child on somebody's doorstep wasn't a normal thing to do, and it certainly wasn't right. Even if Eli was well taken care of prior to this, abandoning a child was a crime. She ought to get on the phone to the police right now, try to track down the person who'd left him.

But given her own background, she couldn't be that black and white about the whole situation. Just seeing that backpack sitting on the floor sent her back to the times she'd had to move with only as much as she could carry.

Clearly, she and Will needed to talk about what to do, but it would be best not to do so in earshot of the child.

Allie glanced at the container of leftovers she'd brought over. "Do you have any food a kid could eat?" she asked Will. "Or I can heat up this leftover burger I brought home."

Will tilted his head to one side. "Can a kid eat a burger?"

She looked up at him. Wow. He really

knew nothing about kids. "Haven't done a lot of babysitting, have you?"

He didn't laugh. Instead, he turned to the cupboard and opened it. "I have Marshmallow Crunch cereal," he said. "Or peanut butter and crackers." He pulled out a cellophane-wrapped pack of peanut butter and crackers, and a colorful box of cereal. He brought them over to the table. "Which do you want?" he asked Eli, holding them up. "Or you can have a hamburger."

"All!" Eli's eyes sparkled.

"Uh..." Will looked at Allie, eyebrows raised in a question.

"Choose just one for now," Allie said to Eli.

He pointed toward the cereal.

"Good choice," Will said. He pulled out a bowl and started pouring cereal into it.

"Why do you have that kind of cereal?" Allie asked him.

He winced. "It's my favorite snack," he admitted. He set the bowl in front of Eli, poured milk.

Allie needed a way to keep Eli occupied while they talked. Which probably meant technology. She found a video of dachshund puppies on her phone and put it in front of the child. Immediately, he started scarfing down the cereal, watching the video.

She stood and took Will's hand, tugging him toward the doorway. "Come on," she said. "We need to talk."

His hand was hard, callused. Enough that it startled her. Aside from her brothers, how long had it been since she'd touched a man?

But she knew how long it had been: six months. And it was going to be a lot longer. As soon as they reached the hallway outside the kitchen, she dropped Will's hand. She stood where she could keep an eye on Eli. "What's going on?" she asked Will. "Do you know this kid or why he was dropped off?"

Will blew out a breath and rubbed his neck. "The letter says he's my son."

"What?" Shocked, she spoke too loudly.

Eli glanced back at them. Then he looked at the video again and continued eating.

"*Is* he your son?" she demanded.

Will lifted his hands, palms up. "I mean... I never heard of him until now."

"Could he be?" she asked. How could you have a child and not know it?

"Yeah, I guess." Will was rubbing the back of his neck again.

"You *guess*?" This was unbelievable.

Will was staring through the doorway at Eli. "I haven't always made the best decisions," he said.

"Like using birth control?" She glared at him.

"I've always tried to be careful, but we all know it can fail. Look, I don't know. I have to admit there's a possibility he could be mine, but I can't take care of a child." He looked completely overwhelmed.

Allie held out a hand. "Let's see the letter."

He handed it to her and she skimmed it, then turned it over and read the back. "She says she's sick, and that's why she's passing care of him over to you."

"What?" This time, it was Will's voice that was loud. Quickly, they both looked into the kitchen. But Eli ignored them.

"Didn't you read the back of the letter?"

"No, I guess not. I'm in shock." Will

leaned his head back against the wall as if he needed the support.

Allie continued perusing the letter. “She says she wants Eli to have a chance to grow up with a family member. If you won’t take him, you’re to put him in foster care.”

Allie swallowed hard as the words brought forth memories from her own childhood. Foster care had been a constant threat, and she’d been dumped into temporary care briefly a couple of times before the final abandonment. She wouldn’t wish that on any child. “You need to at least try to keep him, Will,” she said.

“But he might not even be mine.”

“True,” she said. “You can do a DNA test, but for now… keep him. Let him keep his dog.” She remembered all too well having to leave her cat behind when her parents had finally dumped her.

She read the rest of the letter. “She says she’s been preparing him. Having male babysitters for him, weaning him from her so he’s not as attached, talking you up. She says he’s an easy kid and you’ll do fine.”

“She’s wrong,” Will said, shaking his

head back and forth. “I don’t know how. And kids... they upset me.”

Allie rolled her eyes. “Kids *upset* you?”

He nodded. “Had a few experiences.”

“If you can’t handle kids, then you shouldn’t be sleeping around,” she said.

“I don’t,” he said quickly. “Not anymore.”

She couldn’t believe she was having this conversation with a virtual stranger. “Look, you have to keep him,” she heard herself say. “I’ll help.”

“No,” Will said. “No, if he *is* mine... regardless, it’s not your responsibility. I think foster care is the better route.”

“It’s not,” Allie said firmly.

“But you saw. I’m inept. I don’t even know how to take care of a dog.”

Right, the dog. “He needs food and such. Let’s look through the backpack.”

Eli was still eating cereal, but his pace had slowed, and his eyes looked droopy. Allie picked up the backpack and carried it out to the hall, setting it on the table by the door. There was a baggie of dog food, a few snacks, clothes, and paperwork. Attached to the baggie of dog food was a note. “Gus needs diet food for his weight. Dachshunds can have back problems."

She showed it to Will. "This person—Eli's mom, I guess? She seems very thoughtful. Why didn't she just come to you?"

"I don't know," Will said. "I don't even know who she was."

Once again, Allie rolled her eyes. "Think back. He's five, so about six years ago. How many girlfriends did you have?"

She glanced in at Eli. He had climbed down to the floor to sit by the dog. He was leaning against a table leg and holding the phone, watching the video.

"Six years ago was the last summer I was here," he said. "I did a lot of drinking and partying, and there were a few women. I'll try to figure it out, but right now, my mind's a blank."

"If there's even a chance he's yours, you're keeping him," Allie ordered.

Will met her eyes. "For tonight," he said. "Only if you stay over."

"Stay over?" Allie blinked.

"I have no idea how to handle him, and you're already establishing a connection."

She looked over at the sleepy child and compassion washed over her. Eli was an innocent, and Will was clearly inept. “Okay. I’ll stay for tonight.”

What was she getting herself into?

5

Will woke up to the smell of bacon frying. For a moment, he was a kid again, staying in his grandparents' house—the most stable, warm family atmosphere he ever had, given his family's itinerant, military lifestyle. They'd rarely stayed in one place for more than a couple of years, and while there had been good things about moving around, he'd always welcomed the sense of home he found here on Orchard Valley Farm.

Surprisingly close, there was a deep bark. Will jolted upright, and it all came flooding back.

Gus, the dachshund. Allie downstairs. Eli, possibly his son.

Gus looked at him, head tilted to one side, and then barked again. Will walked over to the bedroom next door and checked on Eli.

The boy was curled on his side, hugging his stuffed teddy bear, breathing evenly. One pajama-clad leg was out from under the covers. For a moment, Will's heart tugged toward the sweetness, the innocence.

Eli might be his son.

He'd never thought he'd have a child. Didn't want to and wasn't suited to it. But faced with the situation… yeah. It got him right in the heart.

He splashed water on his face and brushed his teeth. A cold nose nudged his leg in a "hurry up" kind of way. He looked down at the dachshund. Little guy must want to go outside, so Will trotted downstairs.

There was Allie in the kitchen, flipping bacon and scrambling eggs—and, Lord, did it all smell good.

"Gotta take the dog out," he said, and went out the back door. It was a cool morning, with drops of dew sparkling on each blade of grass. Gus did his business, and then they both came back inside.

"Thanks for fixing breakfast," he said to Allie. "You didn't need to cook. I didn't expect that."

"I figured if I didn't cook something, we'd all be eating marshmallow crunch for breakfast." She smiled. "Besides, I love breakfast. I had all the stuff at my place, so I ran over and got it this morning."

She was pretty—hair tucked behind her ears, face clean and completely free of makeup. A lot of women would have freaked out about the whole situation—Will himself was freaking out—but she seemed to be taking it in stride.

"I appreciate your staying here, but I still feel bad you slept on the couch," he said. "You would have been welcome to take my bed."

"It's okay," she said. "Somehow, I think my brother would feel better having me sleep on a different floor than you men."

There was a movement in the doorway, and Will turned to see Eli coming in, dressed in shorts and a T-shirt that looked to be on backward.

"Morning, buddy," Will said. "Come here. Let me fix your shirt."

Eli hesitated and then came over to him. When Will reached for him, though, he backed away. Beside him, Gus growled.

The child had slept through the night, surprisingly enough, but he was obviously still uncomfortable with Will getting too close.

"Why don't you set the table, Will, and I'll help Eli fix his shirt," Allie said.

She did so deftly and with no objection either from Eli or the dog. That wasn't surprising. Most babysitters and preschool teachers were women. No doubt a lot of kids were more comfortable with them.

Allie served the food up on the plates Will had set out. He poured orange juice for all of them.

Eli ate eagerly. Will did, too. The bacon was crisp, the scrambled eggs light, the biscuits steaming, quickly melting the butter Will slathered on them. Will had never expected to be sitting at a breakfast table with a woman and child, but here he was—playing, just a little, at having a family.

A few minutes later, Eli wiped off his

mouth. "Mom said you'd take me the first day."

Will looked at him blankly. "Take you where?"

"To school," he said.

Will stared from Eli to Allie. "Does it start today?"

Inside he was reeling. Eli seemed to expect that Will would act like a father, take care of him, take him to school. That smacked of this being Eli's permanent home. Obviously, those expectations had been set by his mother, and they were completely wrong. But it was hard to say so to a five-year-old.

"That's right, I think school does start today," Allie said. "Some of the kids over at Abbott Farm were talking about it. Let me look it up." She pulled out her phone and started searching.

"I'm scared," Eli admitted. He slid off his chair and pulled Gus, who'd been lying watchfully beside him, into his lap.

Something made Will want to comfort the little boy. "Kindergarten's a big step," he said. "But your mom's letter said you were ready for it."

"School is really fun," Allie said. "I used to be a kindergarten teacher, and I know they always do a lot of games and songs on the first day. Which is today," she added, waving her phone at Will.

"Will you take me?" Eli asked Allie.

Allie looked at Will, eyebrows raised. "I do need to meet with a couple of the teachers over at the school anyway," she said. "And I wouldn't mind showing my face at the office, too. I need to spread the word about Abbott Farm's field trip program. I don't mind coming along, if it's okay with you."

"It's okay." Will guzzled the rest of his coffee, his mind racing. If nothing else, he supposed that school might serve as a day-long babysitter while he figured out what to do with this very strange situation. With this child.

Outside, a school bus drove by, and Allie checked the time on her phone. "It's probably time to go if we're going," she said.

Eli nudged Gus off his lap. "I'll be back later, be good," he said to the dog. Then he looked up anxiously at Will and Allie. "Will you take care of him?"

"Of course," Allie said. "He'll be fine."

Will hoped the dog was used to staying inside and wouldn't chew up the furniture or use the floor as a bathroom. But a little dog mess was the least of his worries.

At the school, more surprises awaited. When they walked in, the secretary smiled at Eli and greeted him as if she knew him. Then she looked at Will. "You're his guardian? Will Burton?"

Will felt paralyzed, but Allie nudged him, and he nodded. "Yep," he said. "I'm Will Burton."

"Good. I have a couple of forms for you to sign off on, and then you can take Eli to his class. He's only a couple minutes late."

Will signed his name without reading the forms. He couldn't focus on the words, and he figured they didn't represent some binding contract that he couldn't get out of—not at an elementary school. There would be time enough to straighten it all out later.

They walked with Eli down to Room Six. Will tapped on the door and opened it.

The teacher, a perky redhead, smiled over at him. "Hi, Eli," she said. "Come on in. Do you remember where your desk is?"

Eli nodded, straightened his back, and walked inside.

For some reason, the sight of Eli walking past all the other kids, chin up, hair rumpled, made Will's throat constrict.

The teacher smiled at Will and then gently closed the door as if she expected it would be hard for Will to leave Eli in her care. Little did she know he'd only met the child last night.

And then he was standing in an empty hallway with Allie.

"This is bizarre," he said. "His mother must have enrolled him in this school. And given them my name. Apparently she's been planning this for a while."

"And she must have brought him to kindergarten introduction day," Allie said. "If it's like where I worked, that was probably last week. The teacher already has a desk for Eli, and she knows him."

"Unbelievable."

"It is," Allie said. "Well, I've got to go meet the fourth-grade teacher while she's in her planning period. Then I'll walk over to town and get some things done. Do you mind picking me up when you pick up Eli?"

"Uh, sure." Will's head was spinning. "What time will that be?" He pulled out his phone. He needed to note everything down.

Allie gave him a pitying smile. "You'll have to ask at the office." She took his phone and punched in her number. "Just text me what time, and I'll meet you outside the school. Good luck!"

As she walked down the hall, Will felt like saying, *Wait! Don't leave me!*

But this wasn't Allie's responsibility—it was his. His problem, and he had to figure out what to do about it.

As he checked the school hours with the secretary and made sure that Eli would have something to eat for lunch, as he made a scheduled visit to a nearby farm to pick up a couple pieces of vintage equipment, as he drove back to Orchard Valley Farm, he turned it all over in his mind. What to do. What to do. What were his options?

His thoughts flip-flopped, back and forth.

He was uncomfortable with children. Ever since what had happened to Imad, he'd avoided them. He hadn't seen the danger coming. It would be best to avoid the risk.

But little Eli was so brave. How could

Will turn down caring for Eli based on his own discomfort when a five-year-old was facing up to his own challenging situation with courage?

Besides, who knew if Eli was really his child?

What if he is? If that was the case, then it was Will's responsibility. And you fulfilled your responsibilities. That was what his grandparents had taught him, and Will believed it.

One option was to place Eli in foster care immediately. Probably, social services would take him if they knew the situation.

But Eli had already been abandoned once, last night. Now, he was in a school he'd been told he'd attend.

If the child went into foster care, more than likely, he wouldn't be placed in this school district. And as they discussed last night, there was no way Eli could take his dog along.

He unloaded the equipment and carried it into the barn, pondering. Started sanding the rust off an antique blade, and as always, the work calmed his mind and brought some kind of clarity.

He remembered the summer in question —not entirely, but in flashes. Now, he was embarrassed that he'd partied so much he didn't know for sure whom he'd been with, but there it was. He'd been young and stupid.

He could narrow the possible mother down to a couple of women, or at least he thought so. He'd asked Eli his mother's name, but Eli had just shrugged and said "Mommy." The school might have her name on record, but if he asked, he'd be revealing how little he knew about his own child. Maybe they'd start questioning Will's right to custody, and while he had his own doubts about his ability to parent Eli, he didn't want to have the opportunity taken away. Didn't want Eli to face another change of guardianship.

He was going to have to talk to Stone about the situation. Stone and he had run around together, and Stone might be able to either confirm his suspicions as to who it was or suggest other options.

He also needed to research the legalities of the situation. It didn't seem kosher to leave a child on someone's porch, even if that someone might possibly be the child's other parent.

So before he went to pick up Eli after school, he was going to spend some time on his computer, finding out about custody and guardianship. While he was at it, he'd also order a DNA kit.

Will had come home to Orchard Springs to find peace and solitude. But there was no peace and no solitude. Was he even going to be able to handle this, given his mental state?

He wished he were a praying man, because he could use some help—and soon.

6

The afternoon of Eli's first day at school, Allie paced back and forth in front of the coffee shop where she had spent several hours working. She was beat.

After talking with a couple of teachers and confirming that most of this year's field trips were already planned, she'd expanded her idea for a teacher-centered open house to one that welcomed the entire community. She'd interviewed two potential part-timers to staff the farm-visit program. And she'd drafted a brochure to distribute in the surrounding towns, letting teachers and parents know what was available for their kids at Abbott Farm.

Having a farm-visit program was wonderful, and she was thrilled to have the job, thrilled that Pop Abbott and her foster siblings wanted her to develop and run the program, especially since she hadn't succeeded in getting a kindergarten teaching job here.

At the same time, it was a lot of responsibility. She was realizing that more and more. Now, she just wanted to go home and relax.

In fact, she wanted to go *home* home, not to Will's farmhouse. She had yet to set up her tiny house in the cozy way she envisioned. Instead, the kitchen was half unpacked and boxes filled the little living room. She hadn't even set up her bed.

That wasn't the only reason she didn't want to stay longer at Will's farmhouse. She needed to extricate herself from the father-son situation. It wasn't her responsibility to care for Eli. That clearly belonged to Will. On the other hand, it *was* her responsibility to make the farm visit program a success. She needed to focus on that. She had a lot to do if she was going to get everything set up in time for a few test field trips later this fall.

She checked the time on her phone. Will had texted that he would be there in five minutes, but it had been fifteen. She wasn't surprised. Probably he hadn't anticipated things like the car line and talking with the teacher that went along with picking up a kid from school, especially the first day. He really was pretty clueless about life with kids.

A few shoppers walked along Main Street, going into the hardware and the bookshop. In the distance, she heard a couple of school buses chug by. No Will, though, not yet, so she continued to pace and think.

In addition to wanting to focus on her work, she needed to escape the coziness of being in the farmhouse with Will and Eli. She couldn't help slipping into the mom role: cooking, cleaning up, nurturing. She had always longed to be a wife and a mom. But that wasn't going to happen for her. She wasn't the type of woman men stayed with; she was the type they toyed with and then dumped. That was what her single serious dating experience had taught her, and it paralleled what had happened to her as a kid, in her family. Her parents hadn't stuck around, either.

So Allie needed to stop teasing herself with the fantasy of having a family. Being in Will's farmhouse was like being a dieter in a donut shop. Why torture herself with what she couldn't have?

She had a wonderful found family in the Flock. She needed to focus on that and forget about the rest of it.

Will's truck pulled into the parking space in front of her. As she headed toward the passenger door, though, Will got out. "I need to pick up a couple of things at the hardware store," he said. "Is that okay?" He seemed to assume it was, heading to the back seat and getting Eli out of the spanking-new car seat he had apparently just bought.

She sighed. "Sure, that's fine." Then she perked herself up to give Eli a cheerful greeting. He smiled wanly but didn't answer. Poor kid was probably exhausted.

They walked into the hardware store and were immediately assailed with the smells of fertilizer, oil, and freshly cut wood. The place was packed to the gills with all kinds of tools and supplies. Allie didn't have an inkling of what most of them were for. But it was colorful, and Eli seemed to like it, coming out of his tired shell a little bit and smiling.

As soon as they were inside, the store proprietor, Mr. Martell, hurried over. He must have recognized Allie as being connected with Stone. A few months ago, he'd been inexcusably rude to Stone, and several of them had gone to talk to him about it, Allie included. They'd worked it all out, but clearly, Mr. Martell was still on his best behavior with the Flock or anyone connected.

"How can I help you?" he asked.

Will started talking about some long bolts he needed, and Mr. Martell nodded and gestured for Will to follow. Good. Allie would tell Stone that Mr. Martell was being nicer.

Meanwhile, she occupied herself and Eli by looking at the stuff on the shelves. They spent a little time by the birdseed and feeders, then moved on to the paintbrushes and cans of paint.

Mr. Martell and Will must've gotten to talking. This was taking longer than she'd expected. Finally, Allie pulled a handful of paint swatches down and handed them to Eli, hoping he would find them entertaining.

Eli grabbed them all, tossed them in the air, and laughed as they scattered to the ground. Then he started running to the end of the aisle and back to her. No wonder. He'd been cooped up in school all day. She knelt and picked up as many of the paint swatches as she could, then backed out of the aisle and stood on tiptoes, trying to see where Will and Mr. Martell had gone.

All of a sudden they came around the corner, startling her. Next to Mr. Martell, Will looked even taller and broader and more handsome than he had before.

Her face heated at the thought.

"Stop!" Mr. Martell yelled suddenly, looking down the aisle. Allie spun to see that Eli was climbing the shelves like a little monkey. He was already up at shoulder height. He could get hurt.

She ran toward him, Will rushing beside her. Will grabbed Eli from behind, and Allie loosened his fingers from their death grip on the shelf. "Down you go," she said in a peppy voice, hoping to keep Eli from getting upset.

There was nothing peppy about Mr.

Martell, though. He marched over, knelt down in front of Eli with some difficulty, and started scolding the boy.

Will spoke to her quietly. "I thought you were watching him."

"I thought you were having just a quick visit here," Allie retorted.

Eli turned away from Mr. Martell and threw himself down on the floor, kicking and screaming in a full-scale meltdown. The kid's voice was loud enough to pierce eardrums throughout the store.

Allie was more concerned about keeping Eli safe. She hurried to put her jacket beneath Eli's head in case he started banging it down on the floor. That was often the next step in a five-year-old's tantrum.

What had they expected after Eli's first day of kindergarten? They should never have brought him on an errand.

Mr. Martell got to his feet, shaking his head.

Will leaned over and got in Eli's face. "Hey! Stop that right now."

He didn't really look angry, but his voice was sharp and he was frowning.

Eli screamed louder and thrashed harder.

When Will paused, looking like he was at the end of his rope, Allie knelt beside Eli. She rubbed his arm back and forth, slowly. When the child stopped for breath, she leaned close and spoke in a low, calm voice. "Hey, hon, you need to settle down. We can't go home until you stop."

For a moment, Allie thought that might be enough, but Eli continued screaming loudly.

She checked that the jacket beneath his head was protecting him and then stood and stepped away.

Will started to scold some more, but Allie put a hand on his shoulder and beckoned for him to stand. When he did, she said, "We may just have to let this pass."

"Let it pass? Let him think this is okay?" Will looked at her as if she were out of her mind. So did Mr. Martell, who was standing like a short angel of judgment over the whole situation, arms crossed, expression disapproving.

These men might think they could intimidate Eli into silence, but they didn't know kids like she did. She ignored Mr. Martell and addressed Will. "Think of the past twenty-four hours for him. He got left at your house, slept in a strange environment, and had his first day ever of school. It was our mistake, bringing him on an errand after the first day of school."

"I didn't know," Will said defensively, as if his ignorance was her fault.

She raised an eyebrow and glared at him.

"I didn't know," he said in a quieter voice. "There's a lot I don't know. I'm sorry."

Eli's cries were lowering in volume. He wasn't kicking as much, either. His cute little face was red and wet with tears. Poor kid had to be exhausted.

Will studied him almost helplessly, then seemed to pull himself together. He addressed Mr. Martell. "Let me pay for this stuff while Eli settles down," he said. "Then we can leave you in peace."

The two men headed toward the counter at the front of the store.

Eli wasn't yelling now, just crying quietly. Her heart went out to him. She knelt and pulled him into her lap, and he clung to her, his thumb in his mouth.

She swayed back and forth. "Okay, okay. You're okay." Her heart was melting.

After a moment, she pulled away from him long enough to stand. He reached up his arms to her, and she held her own arms out and told him to jump. His landing made her stagger. He wrapped himself around her like a monkey, and she walked slowly to the front of the store.

He was not a small child, and he was heavy. She couldn't carry him for long. But the feel of a child's arms around her, the weight of him, opened a well of longing in her chest.

Will had paid for his supplies and was waiting at the door. He reached out to take Eli, but the boy clung to Allie.

"You're gonna have to walk then, kiddo," she said. "Down you go." Between them, they got Eli to stand on his own two feet. They walked out toward the truck. Eli still clung close to Allie, clutching her leg.

When they finally reached the truck, Allie lifted Eli in and fastened the buckles of his car seat. When she turned to climb into the passenger seat, Will held out a hand to help her. He didn't let go but pinned her with his eyes. "I know it's a lot to ask," he said, "but can you stay another night?"

Allie thought of her desire to get her place settled, to sleep in her own bed. Even to just set up her bed.

She glanced back at Eli. He was staring up at her with big, teary eyes, and her throat tightened. "Of course," she managed to say.

"Thank you," Will said. "I really, really appreciate it."

As they headed back to the farm, Allie put down her window and breathed in the country air and wondered how it had come to this.

She had wanted to get herself out of this father-son dynamic, but Will and Eli had foiled that goal. So now she was committed to another night of playing family.

7

Will's own shouting woke him up.

Around him, flashes of light, running people, fellow soldiers and civilians, smoke from an explosion, a child crying. He struggled to respond, to help, to save the child, but something was restraining his arms and legs.

"Will! Will, wake up!"

He opened his eyes. The chaos faded, and he focused on a concerned face above him.

"Allie?" He grabbed her arm and held on. The feel of her soft skin was a lifeline, pulling him back to the present.

"You had a dream," she said.

Will's heart was pounding hard enough that it was about to explode his chest. His sheets were soaked with sweat.

Sheets. Allie. A dream.

The smoke, the noise, the flashes faded. He looked around.

He was in a bedroom. The bedroom of his grandparents' house. It was Tuesday night, or more likely, Wednesday morning.

He lay still, breathing hard, trying to collect his thoughts. Everything was okay. He wasn't in a firefight. There wasn't a child he needed to save.

Only... he could still hear a child crying. And a dog barking. He shook his head, trying to dislodge the sound.

"Will, are you okay?"

He blinked and looked at Allie, whose forehead was creased with concern. "Yeah, I'm okay. I'm sorry."

"Can you let go?" She tapped his hand that was still encircling her arm. Squeezing it, really. Way too hard.

He loosened his grip immediately, pulled his hand away. There was a red mark. He had probably bruised her. He propped himself up on his elbow, looking fully into her eyes for the first time. "Oh man, I'm sorry."

Even as he spoke, flashes of the dream kept coming back to his mind.

She nodded, her expression gentle. "It's okay. I'm going to go check on Eli now. He's crying."

"Go," he said. Then he lay there as his heartbeat slowed back down and the sweat dried, making him cold.

He'd hurt a woman and terrified a child... in his sleep. This was why he didn't live with anyone.

He hadn't had a dream for a month or longer, and he'd hoped that they were over. All the therapy he'd done had helped. The dreams had decreased in frequency, from every night to a couple of times a week to once a month or less.

But, he remembered, his therapist had warned him that changes in his life could bring back the more intense manifestations of PTSD, including the nightmares.

In the past couple of days, he'd had nothing but changes, including the change from solitude to living with two other people, at least temporarily.

Including learning he was a father… maybe.

As the sound of his breathing lessened, he heard Allie's low voice, murmuring. Eli was still crying, but in sporadic bursts, not constantly.

Will took deep breaths, the box breathing he'd learned in therapy. Slow breath in. Hold. Slow breath out. Hold.

He needed to calm down before dealing with anything, especially Eli.

In the hall bathroom, he splashed water on his face and then looked in the mirror. His face was haggard, and his hair, damp with sweat, stood half on end.

What a look. Belatedly, he realized he didn't even have a shirt on. He grabbed one from the back of the bathroom door and walked out into the hall, where Allie's calming voice was more audible. He didn't hear any more crying or barking.

He tapped on the frame of Eli's door. "Hey, kiddo, you okay?"

Eli was in his bed, looking so small. At the sound of Will's quiet words, he cringed back. Beside him, Gus shied away too, tail between his legs.

Will winced. How could he be a father if his kid was terrified of him?

He forced himself to go inside anyway. Yes, he'd been flipping out and was still feeling the aftereffects, but he had a child to care for, to calm. He sat down on a child's wooden chair he'd found in his grandparents' attic and brought down. He scooted to where Eli could see him, but not too close to the bed, hoping the small chair would make him seem smaller, less intimidating. As long as he didn't break the thing.

For the first time, he noticed that Allie was wearing a long cotton nightgown, white and lacy. It was striking with her dark coloring. She looked like an old-fashioned vision.

She was speaking quietly to Eli. "Mr. Will had a bad dream," she said.

"He's not Mr. Will, he's my dad," Eli said in a clear, high voice.

Whoa. Will stared at the boy, his mind racing. This was the first time he'd heard Eli say anything of the sort, and anger toward Eli's mother rose in him. What kind of idea was Eli going to get about fathers if this didn't work out? Way to set the child up for disappointment.

His heart rate accelerated again, his fist clenching. When Allie looked pointedly at it, he realized his adrenaline was still way too high. He needed to focus on Eli, not on himself. He relaxed his fist and took a couple more deep breaths.

"Sorry I scared you," he said to Eli, mimicking Allie's low, soothing tone. He scooted his chair just a little closer. "I did have a bad dream. But when I woke up, I saw it wasn't real."

Eli nodded, his expression serious. "I have bad dreams sometimes. About a monster..." He yawned. "A monster... under... the bed."

"That would be scary," Will said.

"Uh-huh." Eli's eyes drooped. Gus settled on the bed next to him with a yawn that ended in a little groan.

Allie was gently stroking Eli's arm. "Keep talking," she mouthed to Will.

So Will talked, as quietly and slowly and boringly as possible, about staying here in this house when he was a boy. Sleeping in the very same bed where Eli was sleeping now. The kind of food his grandma had cooked. The books they'd gotten at the library. The creeks where they'd gone fishing.

Eli yawned again, and soon he was breathing evenly. His eyes closed.

Allie looked over at Will and smiled, a dimple denting her cheek. "Good job," she whispered, and they sneaked out.

And then they were standing there in their nightclothes in the hall. Will could smell a floral scent from Allie's hair. He wanted to touch that soft skin. Wanted to clasp her to him.

Inappropriate. He took a step back.

"I don't think I can sleep quite yet," she said. "I'm going to fix myself some tea and read a little. Want some?"

Will knew he wouldn't sleep. He didn't want to go back to sleep and risk another dream. "Tea would be nice," he said. "And I'll grab a book. I finished mine last night."

Downstairs, she put on the kettle for tea. The light was low, golden, and the windows were dark, shining surfaces, with nothing visible outside. He looked up at the old-fashioned kitchen clock—2 a.m.

"I'm really sorry I woke you," he said.

"It's okay," she said. "You couldn't help it."

"I'm glad you were here," he said. What would have happened if she hadn't been? Would he have gone on dreaming, freaking out, making noise? Terrifying the five-year-old in the room next door?

"I'm glad I was here, too." She handed him the tea.

He wanted to ask her to stay longer, but he hesitated to do that. Now probably wasn't the time, and anyway, he didn't know if it was going to be necessary. Didn't know if Eli would stay.

"Do you have a lot of dreams?" Allie asked.

He dunked his teabag. "Not so often anymore, but that one was a doozy. My therapist warned me that changes in my life might bring them back."

"You've had a lot of changes, for sure," she said. There was compassion in her eyes, sympathy in her voice.

Their eyes met.

She looked away, sipped tea. "Have you figured out who the mom is? And if you're really Eli's dad?"

"Not yet. I requested expedited lab results for the DNA test and should get them back in another day or two." He hesitated. "I have an idea who the mom could be."

He'd talked to Stone and looked through some old pictures from the summer in question. He'd seen in them a pretty girl he'd slept with a couple of times when she'd been visiting her aunt and uncle.

He regretted the casualness now. Wouldn't do that again. As he recalled, she'd been equally casual, just visiting town for a couple of weeks, not wanting anything serious.

But if it was true that Eli had come of the union, then the result of their short fling had been extremely serious.

He had searched for her online and tried to contact her, but her last available address was in California. Her phone was disconnected, and there was no email or alternate number.

He told Allie the rough outline of what he'd discovered. He worried that she'd be shocked about the short-lived affair, but she didn't flinch. "Could you talk to her family?" she asked. "Find out if she got married, changed her name?"

"Maybe." He wrapped his hands around

the teacup. "I think I'll need to hire a detective and find out at least something about her, if it proves true that I'm the dad."

"Wonder why she wouldn't want to be found."

"No clue." They'd parted on good terms, as he remembered. They'd lost touch, but obviously, she'd kept tabs on his location. She'd had a reason to: his baby.

But why wouldn't she have contacted him for child support, at least?

He sipped tea, put his cup down, ran his hands through his hair. "I tell you what, Allie, life can go in pretty unexpected directions."

She nodded. "It can," she said quietly. She stared into her teacup.

"Has yours?" he asked.

"That's a subject for another time." She took a breath, drank down the rest of her tea, and stood. "Time to read myself to sleep," she said.

"I'll try for that too." He stood and stepped closer. There was that flowery fragrance from her hair again. "Thanks for the tea and talk. And thank you for being here. You did great with Eli."

"You're welcome," she said with a little smile. "Kids are my area of expertise, after all."

Her cheeks were pink, her lips full. That old-fashioned nightgown of hers covered everything but still managed to tantalize him.

He'd like nothing better than to hold her, kiss her. Because it would chase the demons away, sure, but also because she was sweet and kind and pretty.

She was staring at him steadily. Her breathing quickened.

He reached out, touched her arm where he'd grabbed her before, nodding down at her forearm. "Did I hurt you?"

She shook her head, her eyes wide. "I'm fine."

He leaned a little closer, but warning bells rang in his head and he straightened. He needed to remember who he was, what he'd done.

His new motto was do no harm. And he'd certainly harm innocent Allie if he got close to her.

Apparently, he could harm women and kids in his sleep.

He patted her shoulder awkwardly, then strode to the living room, grabbed a random book from the shelf, and trotted upstairs.

Only when he reached his bedroom and settled back against the wrought-iron headboard did he realize two things. One, he'd grabbed a tattered historical romance novel that had to be at least forty years old, sporting a bare-chested man on the cover.

And two, he actually *hadn't* calmed down, as he'd hoped to do. After the feelings that had surged up about Allie, he was more agitated than ever, in a different but equally dangerous way.

8

On Friday night, Allie was hoping for a nice meal with her family. That was how she thought of the Flock. They'd been found family before that was a thing.

So, everyone was crowded in Pop's farmhouse, jostling one another in the kitchen, banging through the back door for one last game of catch, cranking up the music after a long week. They'd have dinner now, and there was a plan later for a bonfire.

This was what she'd envisioned when she moved back, that she could enjoy time with her family. And time alone, too.

Instead, she was spending too much of

her time with a very attractive but very troubled man and his maybe-son.

Stone shooed everyone away while he pulled pizzas out of the oven. Then everyone had to find a seat and state their preference for milk or soda or iced tea. That took a while, especially since there were kids involved: Stone and Elena's daughter, and Jenn and Eddie's, both around eight. David and Courtney didn't have kids yet, but they were exploring adoption.

As Allie poured drinks, she thought back over the week. It had been busy. She'd spent her days mostly here at Abbott Farm working on getting things set up for school field trips. Amish workers were there building a shelter house, an open-sided building that would hold long picnic tables. That spot was essential for groups of kids to gather: for lunches, to hear instructions, and if it rained.

At the last minute, she'd decided that porta-johns wouldn't work with the age groups they hoped to attract. Too scary for little ones. So she got the Amish workers to do some overtime building a shed that would serve as a bathroom. Then she'd spent hours trying to find a plumber who was willing to put in the facilities on an accelerated timeline. She'd argued with Jenn and Stone about setting aside areas for school buses to park, neither of them wanting to give up parts of their fields for the purpose.

She'd also been working with David on the financials, which was his area of expertise in supporting Abbott Farm. And yeah, he was her foster brother, but he acted more like a banker when they were discussing the expenses of the farm-visit program.

At one point, irritable with his demands that she produce multiple spreadsheets and a formal business plan, she'd balked.

In response, David had gotten very serious. This school-visit program was the final piece of saving the farm for Pop Abbott. All the other endeavors—the farm stand, Jenn's flower field, Stone's organic business—were at least breaking even or set to do so within the first year. The school program needed to do the same as soon as possible.

That had taken her aback and made her think. People were counting on her. This was more than a job. So she'd redoubled her efforts, working long hours and planning to do the same next week.

The nights? They were a different story. So far, she'd spent each one on Will's couch. But there had been no repeat of nightmares for either male in the house, and she was wondering if they might be okay with her sleeping at her own place now. After all, she was just a text message away.

Once everyone was settled around the table, they prayed and then dug in. It was the kind of casual meal Allie loved. There was something festive about pizza, and this batch, made by Stone, was especially delicious. He'd roasted fresh onions and peppers from the farm, and used their own homegrown tomatoes to make the sauce. High-quality cheese melted on top and a thin, flavorful crust.

Yeah. It was delicious, and she told Stone so, making him smile.

They were all talking over each other and all helping the kids and scolding the begging dogs—Courtney's goldendoodle, Bubbles, and Pop's bulldog, Chester. Pop Abbott presided over it all, beaming from the head of the table.

Allie's heart warmed just looking around. This was her family. She wasn't going to have her own spouse and kids like the rest of them, but she knew without question that the Flock would include her in family activities.

She'd be the cool aunt. That was a perfectly good role.

It was after dinner that things went south.

As she and Jenn carried dishes from the table to the sink, Jenn asked her if her new bed was comfortable.

"I don't know," Allie blurted out.

Stone, scraping plates into the trash, overheard. "Why don't you know if your bed is comfortable?"

Allie let her eyes close for a minute. Why had she let that slip?

"Well, because..." She trailed off. She couldn't think of a believable story fast enough, and besides, Stone had always been able to tell when she was hiding something.

"Allie? What's wrong?" he asked in his concerned-big-brother way.

Jenn walked closer and put an arm around Allie. "Yeah, what's wrong?"

Well, it would've come out one way or another, she supposed. So she explained about Will and Eli, Eli's bond with her, Will's PTSD, the nightmare that she'd had to comfort both of them through.

"That must have been awful," Jenn said, sounding distressed. "We could've helped."

Stone crossed his arms over his chest, his eyes narrowing. "I would have helped. But I suspect I know why he didn't ask."

"Why?" Allie and Jenn asked simultaneously.

Stone looked at them as if they were dense. "Because he wanted to hook up with Allie."

"Stone!" Jenn looked embarrassed. The Flock didn't usually get granular in talking about each other's love lives. Allie had never heard Stone say anything like "hook up" before.

She waved off the idea. "That's the last thing he wants."

"Don't be too sure," Stone said, his voice concerned. "He's got you sleeping in his house! It's just a short step to..." He trailed off. "You know what I mean."

Allie found herself blushing, thinking of

that night Will had leaned close and looked into her eyes.

Maybe Stone had a point. But no way was she telling him that. She didn't want to hear his big-brother lecture.

"I'm going to talk to him tomorrow," Stone said. "And you're not to sleep over there anymore."

Jenn and Allie both stared at Stone, then at each other.

"Wow," Allie said finally.

"What?" Stone slammed down a pot he was washing, too hard.

"You don't get to tell her what to do," Jenn said.

"Yes, I do. She's my sister and I'll take care of her." Stone banged another pot down on the counter and looked at Jenn. "When you needed help, I was here. Same with David. And now, if Allie needs me, I'm here for her."

"You always do that," Jenn said, hands on hips. "You always assume you know the right way to help people. And that they *want* your help. Well, news flash: they don't!"

Allie thought about waving a hand in front of them to remind them that she was here and it was her life. Coming home, being with the Flock, was more complicated than she'd expected.

As they continued to argue, she rinsed and dried her hands, then started toward the door. "I'm going to head out."

Stone and Jenn both swiveled and stared at her.

"Wait, what?" Jenn asked.

"Where are you going?" Stone added.

Allie pointed at Stone. "Jenn's right. You don't get to tell me what to do." Then she looked at Jenn. "And thanks for defending me, but I can fight my own battles."

She walked the rest of the way to the door and grabbed her coat, ignoring the offers of rides, the quick apologies, the "what about the bonfire" from Jenn.

"I just need a little time to myself," she told them. And she needed to walk, because that was how she sorted things out in her mind.

Soon she was heading down the country road toward Will's farm. The sun was sinking behind the tree line, and the sky was turning purple. Around her, the birds were singing their sundown songs. A blue jay chattered at her from a fencepost.

"Don't you start," she said to the blue jay. "I've had enough scolding tonight."

Which was ridiculous. She was a twenty-eight-year-old woman, not a child. So where did Stone get off, laying down the law like he was the dad of a young teenager?

Besides, there was nothing to worry about. There had been no repeat of the slightly intimate moment between Will and Allie. Of course there hadn't. A man like Will wouldn't want someone like her. Or if he did, it would be short-term, and then he'd toss her aside.

She didn't want to experience that again. In a deep way, she knew that another abandonment might destroy her. The last one had come close, and she hadn't been truly in love with the man in question. It was just that she'd looked to him for the love she hadn't received from her parents.

But instead of giving it, he'd dumped her. Just like her parents had.

She walked faster, breathing hard. She needed a single, independent life. That had been the plan, moving back to Orchard

Springs. But here she was, in the middle of her interfering family and staying with a hot new man she could never have.

That, she could handle. But there was Eli. She was coming to care about what happened to him. He was a cute kid, like the kids she'd hoped to have someday, if things were different.

And she really, really wanted kids.

Her throat tightened and a tear leaked out of her eye. She backhanded it away impatiently, upping her pace, kicking stones and asphalt from the side of the road.

She inhaled the fragrance of hay and late-summer flowers. She sent up a prayer for help. Slowly, the tension in her shoulders started to ease.

In the distance, headlights appeared. She stepped to the side in case the driver didn't see her. But the vehicle, an old sedan, stopped beside her. The window went down.

A cold hand gripped her heart. Fear was the constant companion of any woman walking through a city at night, but she hadn't expected to feel it out here.

"Allie?"

She looked over, recognizing the voice,

and then confirmed it with the appearance of a balding but shaggy-haired, forty-something man.

Her sort-of brother, Pop Abbott's biological son. "Ronald?"

Ronald had grown up before the Abbotts had started taking in foster children. So he was older than her, probably by twelve or fifteen years. He was a sketchy guy who had done some not-very-nice things in an effort to get control of Abbott Farm and any profits from it. In fact, she remembered as he climbed out of his vehicle, he wasn't even supposed to be around here. The police had let him leave after a recent incident, but with orders not to return or theft charges would be pressed.

And now he was here, and she was alone with him. This night just kept getting better.

"It's good to see you." He reached toward her for a hug, which she dodged with a giant step backward.

"Hi, Ronald," she said, not pretending to be glad he was here.

His fake enthusiasm disappeared. "So where is the rest of your clan, or flock, or whatever you like to call yourselves?"

"They're around," she said. "Most of them are over at the farm, if you want to catch them." She was throwing them under the bus, letting Ronald know where they were, but that beat hanging out with him alone.

"What are they doing tonight?" he asked. "Plotting to take over more of the county?"

He was kind of looming over her, eyes wide, voice comically deep. He used to do similar things to her and Jenn sometimes when they were young teenagers. Being scary in a way that was supposed to be funny, but wasn't.

She'd never gotten an assault vibe from him before, but now... Now, he definitely wanted something. Maybe not her, but information.

"I need to get going," she said, and started toward Will's farm at a brisk walk.

"Wait! Don't go!"

She started jogging. "Got to get my exercise," she tossed back over her shoulder. What was that urge to be nice and avoid conflict? Ronald was a jerk, and he'd been toying with her, getting in her space and acting aggressive. Who cared if he got his feelings hurt?

Her thin-soled tennis shoes hit hard against the asphalt. Her purse was banging against her side. In no way did she look like a runner. Or feel like one, either. She was breathing hard, her muscles protesting the unaccustomed activity.

She didn't hear footsteps behind her. Good. Maybe he'd gotten the message.

But when she glanced back, his car started to move. He executed a U-turn, then pulled up and drove along beside her.

"What are you scared of?" he asked.

"I'm not scared," she said, breathing hard.

But she was. Especially when he swung the car across the road and stopped it, blocking her path.

9

Will paced back and forth on the living room carpet, pausing every few passes to look out the window.

Where was Allie?

The sun had set, and the sky was that deep purple color that preceded the blackness of night. He'd have expected Allie to come home sooner, but there was no sign of her.

Not that she was obligated. She was with the Flock for dinner, and maybe they'd decided to do something else too, causing her to stay longer. That was her right and not his concern.

Or maybe she didn't want to come back because their moment of closeness the other night had freaked her out. She'd continued to stay on his couch for the rest of the week, but she'd come in late and hadn't interacted with him a whole lot, and left early most mornings. Again, that was her right. It was just that, usually, she sent him a brief text letting him know her schedule and plans.

She was doing him a huge favor by sleeping over, making sure he didn't scare Eli with his nightmares. Eli was naturally closer with Allie, it seemed; she was a woman, and she was good with kids. But since she'd been making herself scarce, Eli had gotten more accustomed to Will.

In fact, Eli was adjusting almost too easily. If it turned out that Eli was, in fact, his son, Will would try to get the kid in some kind of counseling, just to make sure he was dealing okay with all the changes and losses in his life.

He trotted up the stairs to check on Eli. The poor kiddo had been exhausted from his first week of school. He'd started rubbing his eyes and yawning at 7:00, and Will had taken him up to bed at 7:30.

Now, he was sound asleep, breathing evenly. Will brushed back his hair and pulled the covers up a little higher. Eli's bear had fallen to the floor, and Will picked it up and tucked it back into the child's arms. Eli slept on.

There was still no word on the DNA results, but Will had to admit he was getting attached. At first, he'd hoped the results would reveal he wasn't Eli's father and that this problem would be quickly removed from his life. Now, it was getting harder to imagine sending Eli away. The child was sweet and brave. Just the kind of son Will would have wanted if anyone had asked.

He went out, shutting the door most of the way, and walked downstairs. He looked out the window of the front room again.

Still no Allie.

His instincts were telling him something was wrong. The back of his neck prickled and his stomach tightened. Wouldn't she have called or texted if she was coming in late?

Will didn't believe instincts were random. Instead, they were a gathering of known and suspected facts, all coming together a little bit beneath one's consciousness.

Something was off about the fact that Allie hadn't shown up and hadn't called.

Will slipped out of the house and looked down the road.

He did see something, but it wasn't Allie. What was that white shape? He squinted and took a few more steps.

A long white car was parked across the road, blocking any traffic that might come.

That wasn't right. Had there been an accident? He jogged toward it. Halfway there, he thought... wait. Eli? But the kiddo was asleep, solidly so. And the car wasn't that far away.

When he reached it, hot rage rose inside him.

Allie was basically penned against the car. A middle-aged man stood just a few inches away, talking at her. Allie looked angry and scared.

Will strode in, grabbed the guy by the arm and the back of his shirt, and pulled him away from Allie, shoving him to the side.

"Hey, what're you doing?" The man sounded indignant.

Will ignored him. "Everything okay, Allie?"

She was breathing hard. She'd stepped away from the car where he'd pinned her, but now, she gripped it again as if she needed the support. "Thanks. No, not really."

"Do you know this guy?" Will nodded toward the other man, who stood off to the side, scowling, rubbing his arm as if Will had hurt him.

"This is Pop Abbott's son, Ronald. He won't let me leave."

"It's not like I'm hurting you," the man said, a slight whine in his voice. "I just need some information about our families."

"And I told you, I'm not talking about the Flock or Pop."

"Who's this guy?" Ronald glared at Will. "Thinks he's some kind of superhero."

"This is Will," Allie said. "He's a friend of the Flock."

Ronald sneered in Will's direction but didn't come closer. "I might've heard about you. Don't you have quite a rep with the ladies?"

Will's eyes narrowed. He wondered what the man had heard, but mostly, he wanted him out of here. "Why don't you head on out, Ronald," Will said. "I don't like how you're acting toward my friend Allie."

"I don't like it either," Allie said. She was backing away, keeping her eyes on Ronald.

Will stepped in front of her, making sure she knew she was protected. "If a lady doesn't want to talk to you," he said to Ronald, "you shouldn't push it." As he spoke, he walked slowly toward Ronald and had the satisfaction of seeing the other man back away.

"But *I* want to talk to *her*!" The whining tone was more obvious now.

"You need to leave her alone." Will stepped closer, deepening his voice and squaring his shoulders, looming over the smaller man.

The intimidation tactics worked. "Fine, fine," Ronald said. He got into his car and squealed away.

Will put an arm around Allie, who was shaking. He tried to let go of his anger toward the man so that he could be gentle toward Allie. "Did he hurt you? Want to call in a police report?"

"No," she said. "I'll call Stone in a little bit, let him know that Ronald is in town." Her teeth were chattering.

He took off his flannel shirt and wrapped it around Allie's shoulders.

"You don't have to do that," she said. "You'll be cold in just a T-shirt."

"I'm fine. You're the one who had the trauma."

"Thanks," she said, pulling the shirt tightly around herself, still shivering. "Where is Eli?"

Eli. Will had momentarily forgotten the child. "Eli is sleeping, but I probably shouldn't have left him alone."

"Let's go," she said, and they hurried back.

They found Eli still sleeping. Beside him, Gus raised his head, then settled back closer to the boy's side.

Back downstairs, Allie collapsed onto the couch. She was breathing hard, and Will was afraid a little bit of shock was setting in. "Let me fix you something," he said. "Tea? Water?"

"Tea would be great. Thanks."

He fixed it and brought it in, along with a bowl of animal crackers that were the only sweets he had on hand. Then he sat down across from her. "What was up with that guy? He seemed like trouble."

"He had all kinds of questions about the Flock. He isn't even supposed to be in this area, I don't think. He got in some kind of trouble a few months ago. He was stealing and trying to manipulate Pop Abbott."

"His own father?"

"He's jealous of the Flock," Allie explained. "He's afraid we'll inherit Abbott Farm. And he's made kind of a mess of his life, so..." She lifted her hands, palms up.

"Well, I'm sorry that happened. Please though, promise me you'll call if you need help or a ride. You shouldn't be walking down a dark road by yourself at night."

"Yeah, you're right," she said. She looked as if she was going to say something else, but she didn't. She just looked at him from under thick eyelashes.

"What's wrong?" He told himself not to look at her in any kind of way except as a friend to protect. But he couldn't help noticing how pretty she was.

Maybe that was what she was wanting to talk about, the odd feelings that had erupted between them the other night.

"It's just... Stone is going to talk to you, I think," she said. "He suspects you're having me stay here because of bad motives."

"Bad motives? Oh." He frowned. "I hope you know I wouldn't—" He broke off.

She nodded quickly. "Oh, I know," she said. She looked away from him, sipped at her tea. "I know you're not interested."

Which was weird, because he had gotten attracted to her, and he was pretty sure she'd noticed. But he *had* pulled back before anything happened, thankfully.

"It's not that..." He stopped. He'd meant to say, it's not that he didn't want her. But that wasn't the right thing to tell her. "I'm just not in the market for any kind of relationship. I let Stone know that when he gave me the warning right before you arrived."

Allie rolled her eyes. "Stone. He's so protective."

Will got it. He wanted to protect Allie too. "We can talk about you not staying here anymore. It might not be necessary as far as me and Eli are concerned. But maybe you want to stay tonight, given that scare with Ronald? You look kind of shaky."

She sucked in a breath, let it out slowly, then nodded. "That would be great. I think I will stay, at least tonight. But you don't have to entertain me."

He nodded. He could use a little distance himself, given the feelings that were starting to kick up again. "I'm going to do a little work on my laptop," he said.

"That sounds great. I have some work to do too. I'll go get mine."

He watched her from the door as she ran over to her house and came back. He didn't think Ronald would come back and lie in wait for her, but you never knew.

Once she returned, he grabbed his laptop, and they settled down into the living room. Both of them with blankets over their laps, tapping on their computers.

It was a little too cozy for Will. He'd saved Allie, which made him feel good. But now he was getting back into having all the feels for her. He needed to focus on his work. He opened his laptop and checked his email, then sucked in a breath—apparently loud enough for Allie to hear.

"What is it?" she asked.

"It's my results," he said slowly. "From the DNA place."

10

Will was up early Saturday morning after a sleepless night. He went into Eli's room and watched him sleep, peaceful, breathing steadily, eyes closed.

Will was a father. Eli was his son.

He padded downstairs alongside Gus, feeling emotional and overwhelmed. There was so much he needed to do now: legal matters, medical checkups, probably counseling for Eli.

He'd been concerned for the boy before, but now, that concern had multiplied. Because it was up to Will to address Eli's problems, make decisions, guide the boy into adulthood.

Will didn't feel that he was fit or suited to be a father, but you couldn't argue with biology. Eli was now his responsibility.

He let the dog out and was fixing a cup of coffee when Allie popped into the room, fresh-faced in a T-shirt and cut-off shorts, no makeup.

She studied him, looking concerned. "You okay?"

He shrugged. "As okay as anyone who just got some terrifying news can be. Coffee?"

"Sure," she said. "And then I'll make pancakes. You look like you could use some comfort food."

She was so sweet. Last night, when he'd gotten the news, she'd hugged him, assured him that he could be a good father, and then left him alone. Just what Will had needed. "You don't have to make breakfast," he said, as he let Gus back inside and poured food into his dog dish.

"But would you eat it if I made it?"

He grinned. "With pleasure," he said.

"Then I'll make it. I love breakfast, and I love to cook."

As she got out pancake ingredients and started mixing them together in a big bowl, Will shared what he'd been thinking. "I don't know where to start," he said. "I'll keep working on connecting with his mother, of course. But now I feel like I have as much responsibility as she does for making decisions about him. I need to find a pediatrician, and talk to a lawyer about legal status, and—"

"Hold on, Will," she interrupted, waving a spatula in his direction. "There's not much you can do until Monday as far as getting him a medical checkup or talking to a lawyer. What's a bonding activity you used to do with your father?"

"A bonding activity?"

"You know. Father-son stuff."

Will thought about that. "We went to a firing range a few times," he said. "Which I'm not doing with Eli."

Her eyebrows shot up. "Oh my goodness, no. He's five! You and your dad didn't do anything else special?"

She was pouring pancake batter onto a

griddle pan, the same one his grandmother had always used. She had the same expression of concentration, the same ability to listen at the same time. Must be a female trait.

"We moved around a lot," he said. "Dad was always busy with his work."

One memory did come to him: his father had taken him out one evening when he was fifteen, had instructed him that he was going to learn to be a man, and had sent him into a hotel room with a very pretty older woman. Only later had he understood that she was a prostitute. It hadn't been a terrible experience—he was a normal adolescent boy with the usual strong urges—but it had left him feeling uncomfortable and embarrassed. Not only because of the woman, who'd actually been kind, but because of having to ride home in the car with his father, afterwards.

That was around the time his parents' marriage had been falling apart, and it had all worked together to push Will in the direction of lots of superficial relationships.

Yeah, no. Not a model he wanted to emulate with Eli. Nor to share with Allie.

Allie put a couple of pancakes on his plate. "Any other father figures?"

That made him brighten. "My grandfather," he said. "That's why I loved to come here."

"Your grandparents will be excited to find out about Eli," she said.

"Oh, they will." He smiled at the thought. Maybe they would come and visit. Maybe Eli could have an extended family.

"What did you do with your grandpa when you visited?" she asked.

An image flashed into his mind, pure and perfect: him and his grandfather on a big flat rock on a local river, his grandpa teaching him to fish. He could see the blue sky, feel the cool air, smell the fishy, earthy scent of the surrounding water. During his worst times overseas, he'd remembered that peace.

He told her about it.

"Why don't you take Eli fishing today?" she asked. The smell of bacon drifted through the air, tantalizing him. He poured them both some coffee and located the pancake syrup.

"That seems irresponsible when there's so much I need to do."

She shook her head. "Bonding is the most important thing at this point."

Her certainty struck him. She was right.

"I haven't been fishing in years," he said. "I don't have tackle, although my grandfather may have some in the shed."

"Pop Abbott has some fishing tackle too. And he'll know where to buy bait and where some good places to go are locally."

"You are the best." He put an arm around her and squeezed, then went back to his seat.

Eli, wearing pajamas, came in and climbed into a chair, rubbing his eyes. "Pancakes!" he said.

"Coming right up," Allie said, and put one on Eli's plate.

Eli's eyes widened. "It's shaped like a dog," he said.

Will looked over and was amused to see that Allie had somehow poured the pancake to make a couple of ears and a nose. "Looks like a pig to me," Will said.

"You're both wrong," she said with a pretend frown. "Can't you see that it's a dragon?"

"That's not a dragon." Eli took a piece of bacon she put on his plate and crunched on it. Will helped him pour syrup onto his pancake. Again, he was struck by the family-like feeling of eating breakfast together. This was a little scary, and he knew he couldn't get used to it. But today, he was going to do as Allie had suggested. He was going to focus on bonding with his son.

"Guess what we're going to do today," he said after finishing another pancake. "We're going fishing!"

Eli frowned. "I don't know how."

"That's okay, I'll teach you." Will felt a little pride mixed with trepidation. He was the teacher. He was going to have to teach Eli a lot of things, and do a better job of it than his own father had done.

"Can Gus come?"

Will imagined the little dog running up and down the lakeshore, barking, scaring the fish. "Not this time," he said. "We'll walk Gus later." It would be more bonding.

"Can *she* come?" Eli pointed at Allie.

"That's up to her," Will said, hoping she would say yes. "She might be busy."

"I have a lot to do," Allie said. "But it's such a nice day. I'll come along and bring a book to read and sit in a chair in the sun. No way am I touching worms."

Will laughed. “That’s fair,” he said.

“I like worms,” Eli said.

An hour later, they were at a dock on a local lake, the sun warming their backs. There were a few other people around, walking the trail around the lake or fishing, but they had this stretch of shoreline to themselves.

Will knelt in front of Eli. “There are rules,” he said. “You have to wear a life jacket. And you have to stay this far away from the water.” He held his hands shoulder-length apart. He was actually channeling Allie, trying to imagine what she would say to a kid she was working with.

Allie gave him a thumbs-up, and Will felt good. He was starting to get the hang of managing five-year-olds already.

He baited a hook and cast out a line for Eli, then showed him how to reel it in. He never realized before how much instruction was needed for fishing, how much help a five-year-old required. Those hooks were sharp, and Eli wasn’t especially coordinated. Gratitude for his grandfather’s cheerful instruction flowed over him. He’d make sure to tell his grandfather the next time they talked.

Allie had done just as she said. She brought a folding chair and a book, and she was perched in the sun, reading. Every now and then, she looked up at them and smiled.

Eli got mesmerized by watching the line and the bobber, and Will looked over at Allie and almost got lost in the sight of her. He was so very grateful for her. If she hadn't been around, he didn't think he could've managed this new development in his life. And she didn't make it seem like she was doing him a favor and incurring debt. She genuinely seemed to like Eli. She even seemed to like Will, flawed as he was.

Behind him, there was a splash, and he spun.

Eli was nowhere to be seen.

"Eli!" He rushed to the edge of the water, his heart pounding hard. If something had happened to the child...

Sure enough, Eli had tumbled in. The water was only about two feet deep, and Eli was wearing his life jacket, but he was still thrashing around and crying.

Will waded in, Allie beside him, and they splashed toward Eli.

Will grabbed Eli and lifted him up, then

wiped his face on the sleeve of his shirt. He carried him to the bank and set him on his feet. It wasn't much exertion, but Will was breathing as hard as if he'd run a marathon.

He knelt in front of the child. "Don't you ever, ever do that again," he said.

Eli started to cry. He was soaked and shivering.

"You knew the rules," Will continued. He had to make Eli understand how serious water safety was. The child could have drowned.

Eli clung to Allie's leg. "I want my mommy," he wailed.

"You're okay, honey," Allie said. She knelt down and hugged him. "Sssh. You're fine. You just got a little wet."

Will tried hard not to look at her figure in the clinging clothes. Her hair was soaked too, but she didn't even seem to notice. She just focused on comforting Eli.

Will sucked in deep breaths, trying to take in Allie's comforting words. Eli was okay. They were all okay. A little water didn't hurt anyone.

But he couldn't regain his carefree status,

and they were all soaked. "We better go home now," Will said.

"I think so too," Allie said.

They gathered their things, packed the car, and drove toward home. Will blasted the heat to help them warm up. Eli quickly fell asleep in the back seat.

Will had been berating himself internally ever since it happened. Now he spoke up. "That was a disaster. I don't know if I can do this."

Allie laughed. "That wasn't a disaster. That was life with a five-year-old. It could happen to anyone."

"He could've drowned."

Allie shook her head. "Maybe there's a one-in-a-thousand chance that he could've drowned. But that's why we had him wear a life jacket. And that's why we stayed on this end of the lake where the water was more shallow."

"I guess," Will said doubtfully.

"Really. Accidents happen with kids all the time. The main thing is that you be the adult and figure out how to fix it."

"Thanks," he said. "For being here and for coaching me."

"You're welcome," she said. "I'm happy for you and Eli." There was a wistful sound in her voice, and he briefly wondered what that was about.

At home, he carried Eli inside. The child woke up a little bit and nestled against him. He was a heavy little tyke, but Will welcomed the weight of him.

He could still feel the terror of when Eli had fallen into the water. Having his weight in his arms reassured him that Eli was okay.

Allie walked beside him, carrying the fishing tackle.

As he got Eli out of his wet clothes and set him down in the bathtub to wash off the lake water, Eli looked up at him. "Sorry, Daddy," he said.

Will's eyes filled with tears that spilled over. Eli had called him "Daddy." Just like that, his heart overflowed with love for this child.

Alongside the love was determination to do whatever was necessary to keep Eli safe and happy.

11

On Monday morning, Allie arrived at Abbott Farm and was dismayed to see that her foster siblings and their spouses hadn't left yet. They were all going to a big Amish farm show about an hour away. The farm stand was closed on Mondays, and the Flock and the spouses had agreed to take the day off for a trip that was half work, half pleasure. Allie had hoped they'd left without her.

"Allie! You're here!" Jenn ran over and gave her a hug, and Allie was ashamed of her bad mood. "You're coming, right?"

"No, I need to get work done." That was true, but she was also tired of her siblings' married-people happiness. Being around three newlywed couples was trying, to say the least. Add in their efforts to matchmake, and Stone's desire to control her, and... yeah. It was all pretty annoying.

David and Stone came over as if her thoughts had conjured them up. "Coming along, aren't you?" Stone asked.

"No, I'm going to stay here and work. I need to get a handle on how ready the farm is for the school field trip program."

David nodded approvingly. "We'll start having school visits soon, right?"

"That'll be great," Jenn said without waiting for Allie's answer. "Another stream of income will take some of the pressure off the rest of us."

"It's kids," David said. "That should be pretty easy, right? Not like the farm-stay adults. They're more picky."

Allie sighed. "Don't underestimate the things that can go wrong with kids," she said. Then, to David, "I'll have a schedule after I do a little more research. Most of the teachers I've spoken with have already scheduled their field trips. We might be able to slide in if some other organization cancels, but no way will anything happen in the next couple of weeks."

Stone looked concerned. "Are you able to focus on this? Do you have too much going on with Will and his kid? Because if you want to come live with me and Elena, you're welcome to." Stone and his new wife were still living in the farm's bunkhouse while the details of the farm-stay program got worked out.

"No, no, I'm fine. Don't you all need to get going?" It was true, their spouses were gesturing and beckoning to them. And soon—but not soon enough for Allie—they were all headed down the road.

Allie pulled out her tablet and started the walk-through she'd been planning. First, the area around the barn where student field trips would arrive. She strolled around it slowly, imagining the day when a couple of yellow school buses would be parked there, the kids spilling out.

She was overwhelmed with her siblings. They were great and she loved them, but they could definitely interfere and boss her too much. Even though she and Jenn were approximately the same age, Allie had always been considered the baby of the group. Which was annoying.

She turned a slow 360 degrees in the parking area where the buses would stop. She was suddenly conscious of the gates that could be opened, the dangling wires that could be grabbed or could cut a careless child. She made note of the hazards to address before inviting any kids to the farm.

In the field beside the barn, a couple of dairy cows mooed a welcome. They were a new addition, and Allie loved their big brown eyes, made charming with long lashes. She walked over and petted one, then wrinkled her nose. They'd been chosen more for friendliness than milk production, and wouldn't be any problem for the kids. Except, yuck. The way kids rubbed their eyes and put their fingers in their mouths... yeah. They definitely needed more handwashing stations.

She'd been watching videos from farm extension services talking about how to get set up with farm school visit programs, and that was a big one. Kids would get dirty, and sanitation was important.

The other thing was programming. They

needed to make the day hands-on. No kid wanted to listen to Stone lecture about organic farming or Jenn rhapsodize about her flowers, unless they had a group of older students who were particularly interested in those topics. They'd lose the little ones by using a lecture format.

No, the kids should get to plant, harvest, do the math of counting out seeds. Read stories about farms. Teachers would want to know what educational objectives were being addressed, would have to submit lesson plans to their administrators before a field trip would be approved. She'd handle some of the teaching herself, but she needed to make sure she had assistants lined up, too.

She circled the barn and walked over to the new shelter house. They'd have to set up some barriers to keep the kids on track or they'd be all over the place. She'd also been doing research on safety, regulations, and insurance, and that all needed to be updated before they could have children here.

She walked out into Jenn's flower field, overwhelmed with the fragrance of lavender. This would be a nice place to bring the kids, have them close their eyes, and say what they smelled. Across the way was a large vegetable garden, and she could imagine that the kids might help harvest whatever was ready in any particular week.

The program was going to be great, but there was way more planning involved before it could become a reality. It was laughable what David had said, that they should be ready soon.

As she looked over her list, she realized she'd have to re-emphasize to the Flock that the school program wouldn't get started this fall, at least not for a couple of months, and even then, not on a regular and frequent basis. There was just too much to do.

She ambled alongside the vegetable garden and back toward the farmhouse. It was a beautiful day, with birds singing in the branches overhead and the smell of rich, fertile earth.

Maybe she could recruit the kids in the family to walk through, and Eli as well. They could be the first guinea pigs to see how things worked. Then they could try getting a small homeschool group to come through, and then, once they'd done their troubleshooting, they could invite the school where Jenn's daughter went—a private school with small classes—to visit for free.

David would be really disappointed, because the project wasn't going to make money for a while yet.

She glimpsed the farm stand off in the distance. Somehow, Courtney and David had managed to make it profitable in the first season of operations. Jenn was headed in the right direction for that with her flowers. And the farm-stay program was almost ready to welcome some fall guests.

Allie was the only one who wasn't contributing. Was she going to fail at this as well as at her old job, her old relationship? True, she hadn't had the time that the others had. She'd been teaching all last year and had only moved here permanently a couple of weeks ago.

As she came into view of the farmhouse, a car pulled up. A familiar car.

Oh no. Ronald.

Her first thought was to call Will. After all, he'd rescued her before. She knew he was out in his barn, working on his restoration projects, which meant he was just ten minutes away. He also had made a commitment to keep his cell phone on, because now he was a dad and needed the school to be able to get in touch with him.

But she didn't want to be all dependent, to call Will anytime she got a little nervous. She could handle this. She stepped back behind the tall corn at the edge of Stone's garden and waited to see what Ronald would do.

"Allie! I know you're here!" he called.

Shoot. He'd seen her car. Maybe he'd seen her.

Well, she didn't want to be dependent, but she also wanted to be safe. She called Will. "Ronald's here at Abbott Farm," she said the moment he answered.

"I'll be right over," Will said.

"I hear you," Ronald was saying. His voice sounded close. Allie took off, running beside the flower field and past the bunkhouse. Ronald was bigger than she was and probably stronger, but he was also older and didn't look to be in the best of shape. If she could make it to the barn, she could hide there.

She dodged behind a big tractor and

then a hay wagon, trying to be as quiet as possible, and finally ended up in the barn.

A moment after she climbed into the hayloft, Ronald came in, huffing and puffing. "You in here? Come on, Allie, I don't mean any harm. I just want to talk to you."

That was probably true, but she still didn't want to be alone with Ronald. She pulled her legs close to her chest and watched through a crack in the floor as Ronald walked through the barn.

The problem was, she was surrounded by hay. Of course, she sneezed.

Ronald backed up and squinted toward the hayloft. "You're up there! I'm coming up."

"No, I'll come down." The last thing she wanted was to get trapped here in a place where there was only one way out.

But when she reached the ladder, Ronald was halfway up. Should she push him down, kick him? She could, and it was the only way to ensure that he wouldn't come up, but she couldn't make herself do it. She really didn't know if Ronald was out to harm her or not. She backed away.

Ronald's head came above the edge of the hayloft. "There you are."

She should've kicked him.

The barn door burst open. "Hey, you. Get off that ladder." It was Will, striding in, scanning the area, tension in every inch of his muscular body.

Allie had never been so glad to see someone in her life.

"Allie?" Will called. "You up there?"

She waited until Ronald had climbed halfway back down and dropped to the floor. Then she scooted to the edge of the hayloft. "I'm up here," she called. Just the sight of Will made her heart rate settle.

Will looked up, and Ronald seized the opportunity to dodge around him and out the door of the barn.

Allie climbed down, and Will met her at the bottom of the ladder. "You okay?"

She sneezed. "Aside from a case of hay fever, yes."

He handed her a set of car keys and went to look out the barn door. Then he beckoned to Allie. "Go on, run to my car. Get in and lock the door. I'll take care of Ronald."

"I'm not leaving you here to deal with him alone," Allie said.

He looked back at her, eyebrows raised. "Allie. It's fine."

It probably *was* a little ridiculous for her to think Will, with his military training, couldn't defend himself. "What if he's armed?"

"Do you think he is?"

She shrugged. "He didn't threaten me with a gun, but who knows? I think there's still a warrant out for his arrest."

Will gave a quick nod. "Call the police and tell them there's a wanted man here."

She called 9-1-1 and started to explain.

Outside the barn, a car engine started. They both looked in time to see Ronald's car squeal away, spitting gravel.

"I got his license number," Will said. "Here. Let me talk to them."

They both ended up talking to the police, walking slowly toward the farmhouse. Once she ended the call, Allie sank abruptly onto the porch.

Will sat beside her, looking concerned. "You okay?" He wrapped an arm around her shoulders, its weight a solid comfort.

"I'm all right." She leaned against him. "Thank you so much for coming. I know this is nothing compared to some of the scary things you've seen, but Ronald freaks me out a little bit."

"Of course." He brushed a lock of hair off her face.

Their eyes met, and then she couldn't stop looking at him. Her breathing quickened.

The sound of another car coming made them jump apart and stand. But it wasn't Ronald coming back. It was Stone.

Allie's heart rate accelerated again for a different and embarrassing reason. It was ridiculous, being afraid of her big brother when she was twenty-eight years old. But there it was.

Stone shepherded Maddie out of the car and toward the farmhouse. "Maddie's sick," he explained. "The school called, and I picked her up early." Then he looked at the two of them with narrowed eyes. "We'll talk later."

Allie's cheeks burned. What must Will think, the way Stone treated her like a child?

And what had she been doing, gazing into Will's eyes, when she was determined to make it on her own?

12

The day after the scare with Allie and Ronald, Will worked steadily, putting the finishing touches on an antique cream separator. He'd gotten all the rust removed, and the gears were operational. Now, it was just a matter of polish.

He had his workshop pretty well set up now, and the doors were thrown open to let in the fresh fall air. Gus had settled into the bed Will had gotten him, a string attached to his collar to keep him from running away.

Each time Will reached out to pet him, though, Gus bared his teeth.

"I could've left you inside, buddy," he informed the dog. “I’m trying to be friendly here.”

Gus just growled.

In the middle of the afternoon, Gus started barking. Will wiped his hands and walked out to greet the car that was pulling up.

“Glad you could come out and pick up the separator,” he said to Sam Thompson. Sam was an old acquaintance, and now he was opening the passenger side and helping his mother out of the car.

“I appreciate you letting us come and see your workshop,” Sam said. “Come on, Mom, I think you’ll like this.”

Sam’s mother didn’t answer, nor did she greet Will. She seemed to be focused on walking over the uneven ground, clinging to her son’s arm. Will knew that she had been diagnosed with dementia and that Sam was her primary caregiver.

When they came into the barn, Will led them to the newly restored cream separator, and the woman’s face lit up.

“I used to crank one of those for Mother!” she exclaimed.

Sam looked shocked. “She hasn’t said but

a word or two at a time in months," he told Will.

The woman was studying the vintage device, smiling.

"It's for you, Mom," Sam said.

The woman gasped, then touched the top bowl's newly shiny side. She put a hand on the crank, then looked inquiringly at her son.

"Go ahead, try it," Sam said. "It works, right?" he asked Will.

Will nodded, and both of them watched while the older woman slowly turned the crank that would send the milk to one spout and the cream to another. A huge smile lit up her wrinkled face.

When the pair got back into the car after stowing the separator carefully in the back seat, Sam's mother was still smiling.

Sam gripped his hand. "Thank you," he said. "This means a lot. To me and to her."

Will's throat tightened as he watched them drive away. This was what he was working for. This was why he loved restoring old farm equipment.

It brought back the past, a simpler time. It reminded older people of the lives they'd had long ago and enabled them to show their children and grandchildren what farming had been like back then.

He went back inside his shop and started working on another project, humming.

He thought about Eli, whom he'd put on the bus this morning. The kid was such a trooper. Will was already proud of him for the way he handled the huge transition he'd undergone. Mindful of what Allie had told him about bonding being the most important thing, Will tried to spend some recreational time with Eli every day. The little boy had warmed up to him some, even letting Will hug him and put him to bed, though he also wanted Allie to comfort him.

Allie. When they'd sat on the porch at Abbott Farm after Ronald had left, when she had thanked Will and looked into his eyes, Will had forgotten every rule he'd made for himself. He'd been so close to kissing her.

And then Stone had pulled up, and they'd jumped apart like they were teenagers getting scolded by the preacher. It was ridiculous.

Why had he gotten himself into that situation, though? Why had he almost kissed Allie again?

Yes, some of it had been adrenaline. But it was more than physical. He felt drawn to her on a lot of different levels. He admired how good she was with kids and her can-do attitude about the new project she was working on. He enjoyed hanging out with her.

And he couldn't let that go on. He needed to stifle it.

He blew the rust off the cast-iron farm bell he'd been working on. Stone would visit any day to harass him more about staying away from Allie. He'd have a hard time convincing Stone that he really wanted to stay away from her when he kept getting close.

Even more important, he worried about Allie. What if she got attracted to him? What if she thought he was interested?

He couldn't let that happen, because it couldn't go anywhere. He couldn't be with a woman. He'd harm her.

Gus barked again, and as if Will's thoughts had conjured him up, there was Stone. He pulled an old hand plow from the back of his truck and rolled it toward Will's barn.

Before the two men could even greet each other, Allie pulled up, jumped out of her little car, and half skipped, half walked to the barn.

She was beautiful. Radiant. Childlike, but all woman. Incredibly appealing.

"Stone, hey," she said, flashing a smile from one to the other. "Will, want me to grab Eli at the bus stop?"

"Sure, that would be great," Will said. He'd been planning to do it himself, but that was before Stone had arrived for a brotherly visit.

After she left, Stone studied Will, frowning. "Look, I know what it's like to be judged by what you did in the past. Or judged falsely, for that matter. But..." He trailed off.

"But you're acquainted with my womanizing ways," Will said.

"Right." Stone let out a sigh. "I like you. I really do. But... when I think about what Allie's gone through in the past... just stay away from her. Find someone else to have fun with."

Will wasn't surprised by the words or the

attitude. Even though he'd told Stone that he'd changed, your actions were what people judged you by, not your words.

And his actions, in regard to Allie, suggested that he hadn't changed. Stone had seen them close to each other, about to kiss. How could Will explain that what he felt for Allie was way different from anything he'd felt for any woman before?

Stone wouldn't believe him. He was nothing if not protective of his foster siblings.

The yellow school bus stopped, and Allie met it and hugged Eli when he came off. Then the two of them walked toward the barn in the sunshine, chatting with animation. The sun behind them seemed to make them glow.

It was everything Will wanted, and it was everything he couldn't have.

"You have my word," he said to Stone. "I'll stay away from her."

13

Almost a week after the scare with Ronald, Allie picked up a plate at the church picnic and surveyed the long table laden with food. It was a beautiful Sunday afternoon, sweater weather now, and the church's shelter house was crowded with people, enjoying the sunshine and eating good church food. Kids played at the creek beside the church or joined in a game of kickball.

It was the best time of year to have a picnic, and some of the church women were very good cooks. Early in September, there was still corn on the cob and salads made with fresh tomatoes. Peach season was almost over, but there was apple pie and cobbler. Pulled pork sent its rich fragrance through the air, mingling with the hamburgers, hot dogs, and veggie burgers being grilled by a couple of the older men.

Allie accepted a burger straight off the grill and walked along the food line, deciding what to sample. But she wasn't just here for the food. She was here to work on her goal of building a rewarding single life for herself.

She'd learned from Courtney, David's wife, that there was an active group of twenty-somethings at the church. It was a singles group, but Courtney had assured her that it was not as much about matching people up as about doing things together.

So, she was determined to join in, get to know people, and get involved. There was only one problem: Will was here, too.

She glanced over to where he knelt beside Eli, pointing at some other kids who were playing together. Then the two of them strolled over to join the group.

Well, wasn't that just so sweet.

After ignoring Allie for days, Will had texted, asking her what church she attended and whether she wanted to ride with him and Eli.

What was she going to say? No, stay away from church?

She knew she had to welcome him as a good Christian. He could use the comfort and support to be found here. Not to mention that Eli needed to be raised with some kind of faith background.

But when they'd ridden here in Will's truck, things had been stiff and awkward between them. He'd escaped ASAP and hadn't sat with her. Now, she wished she hadn't let him know about the picnic after church, hadn't encouraged him to come.

She scooped herself some baked beans and watched as he talked in a friendly way with some of the men. That was good. She'd hoped the church the Flock attended, the church she herself had attended as a teenager, would welcome him.

She couldn't help caring, even though it was no good for her to care. There was no point to it. After rescuing her from Ronald and acting like he wanted to kiss her, he'd dropped her like a hot potato.

Maybe it had something to do with

Stone's visit. Stone was bossy and protective, and no doubt he'd warned Will off.

But if Will cared about her, would he let a few words from her older brother stop him?

No. But the fact remained that he'd dumped her. Which was par for the course with her and men. Thus, the singles group.

She carried her tray over toward the table Courtney had pointed out. "Can I join you?" she asked. She recognized a couple of faces from years past, but didn't know anyone well, not now.

Two women she didn't know smiled and beckoned for her to sit with them, which she thought was sweet—until she saw the avid expressions on their faces. Even before she picked up her fork, they leaned in. "Tell us all about the guy you came here with," one of them said.

"I heard his name is Will Burton," the other woman said. She was forking her fingers through pretty blonde hair. "Are you with him?"

"No!" Allie took a breath and calmed her voice. "He's just a... friend."

"Is he single?" asked one of the women.

"Is that his son?" the other one asked at the same time.

Allie really didn't want to get involved in gossiping about Will, but what was the harm in answering questions? People could find out the truth easily enough. "Yes, he's single," she said. "He's learning to be a dad with little Eli. He just got custody of him."

"Is it true the little boy was left on his doorstep?" the first woman asked.

Allie sighed. She'd sat down hoping to meet some potential friends, but these women were obviously just out for information. "I'm not comfortable talking about him behind his back," she said, meeting the eyes of the first woman, then the other. "If you want to know something about him, you'll need to introduce yourselves and ask him. He's new in town and could use some kind friends." She put extra emphasis on the word "kind."

The women glanced at each other, and the second one had the grace to blush. Obviously, kindness hadn't been the first thing on either of the women's minds.

Allie turned her attention to the rest of the group, talking generally now as they all ate. A perky woman who seemed to be in a leadership role smiled at Allie. "Hi! I'm Ashleigh. We're glad to see a new face. We're planning our fall activities, and we want to get everyone's input."

"Oh? What have you done in the past?" Allie asked, scooting a little away from the nosy duo.

"Oh, we have so much fun, even though we're really just getting started. We've done trips to covered bridges, and we've worked with teenagers, volunteering."

The woman sitting next to her, who seemed to be her co-leader, chimed in. "Maybe we could do a pumpkin patch or a haunted house. Or a hayride. We should embrace the fall vibes."

"How about a corn maze?" someone else suggested. "They're so much fun."

As the others started discussing local places that held fall events, Allie nodded agreement but made a mental note. Could they do a corn maze at Abbott Farm next year? It would be another fun way to get visitors involved. Maybe even the schoolchildren, if it wasn't too challenging. That would be hands on, and could probably be used as some kind of learning experience if she put her mind to it.

"I think we should do a pumpkin patch here at the church, for the kids," one of the women who had been questioning Allie chimed in.

"Oh, that's a good idea," Allie said. "I could help with that. I'm a kindergarten teacher, or at least, I was where I lived before."

"That would be great," the woman in charge said.

The woman who'd suggested the idea nudged Allie. "And you can get your friend Will to come along and bring his son."

That explained her enthusiasm. Allie sighed. "Sure, I can do that." After all, it wasn't as if she was interested in Will herself. Not when he'd feigned interest in her and then dumped her like everyone else.

The talk went ahead to other holiday activities they could do, and Allie forced herself to listen and participate. Most of the group of eight or ten seemed like nice folks, potential friends.

As she finished her meal, someone tapped her on the shoulder.

It was Stone.

He greeted everyone, then leaned forward and asked Allie, "Can we talk a minute?"

"Okay," she said without enthusiasm. She carried her trash and then walked off to the side with Stone.

Stone didn't waste time. "You and Will came to church together."

"Yes. He asked me what church I attended, and when I told him, he offered me a ride. It only made sense to take ride together, since we live next door to each other."

"I wish you hadn't encouraged him to come," Stone said.

Allie took a deep breath and tried to relax her tight shoulders. "It's a friendly church in a friendly town, and he's new. Come on, Stone. Encouraging him to come to church is only Christian."

Stone frowned. "I'm going to have to talk to him. I told him to stay away from you."

"What? Again?"

"Yes, again. I could tell from how close you two were sitting together when I saw you at Abbott Farm the other day..." He trailed off, then spoke again. "Well, I could tell you were starting to have feelings.

"Stone!" Her face heated. "I'm an adult, and I don't need you managing my life! Plus, like I told you, he saved me from Ronald."

Stone shook his head. "Ronald isn't a threat."

"Oh yeah? You try running away from him when you're half his size," she said hotly. "He's the one I need protection from, not Will."

Stone put an arm around her and patted her shoulder. "Ronald's out of town," he said. "I spoke to the police again yesterday. After they warned Ronald to stay away or present himself to the station, no one has seen or heard from him."

"That's the best thing you've told me all day," she said. "But look, Stone, I'm an adult. Please stop interfering in my life."

He looked stricken. "I'm being obnoxious?"

"Yes, you are." She glared at him. "You're also being sexist and patronizing. Cut it out."

"I'm sorry," he said. "I just care about you, and I know what Will's like. He can be a good guy, but he's a womanizer. Always has been. He says he's changed, but I'm skeptical."

"Doesn't matter," she said airily. "I'm not interested."

"Good. Go on, go back to your singles group."

When she started to leave, he pulled her into a quick hug. "Love you, sis," he said.

"I know. Love you too." She couldn't help smiling. Stone was annoying, for sure. But having grown up without a protective family, she appreciated that his bossiness came from caring.

As she headed back toward the singles group, a woman dressed in perfect designer clothes, her hair perfectly coiffed, reached out a hand, stopping her. "Can I speak with you a moment?" she asked.

"Sure," Allie said.

"Great. Have a seat. I'm Lexie, and this is my sister, Sheila. Did I see you arrive with Will?"

"Yes," Allie said, restraining an eye roll. Was everyone obsessed with the new man in town?

"Look, I don't want to be mean, but you should tell him he needs to dress his child better," the woman said. "Someone's going to call social services on him."

"What's wrong with how Eli's dressed?" Allie asked, surprised.

"Well, aside from the fashion disaster, he hasn't got a jacket on."

Allie looked over and noticed that it was true; Eli wore a purple shirt and red shorts. He wasn't wearing a coat, and most of the other kids were. Eli might be a little cold.

Still, she didn't like the way the woman was acting so judgmental. "I'm sure Eli's fine," she said. "If he's cold, he'll tell his father."

"Kids don't always know what they need. It's a parent's duty to dress their kids properly. Do you have kids?"

"No," Allie said slowly, "but I'm a kindergarten teacher."

"Not the same. I'm a mom, and she," she pointed at her sister, "she's the mother of three, so we're more in tune."

Allie blew out a breath. "Since you've noticed the problem," she said sweetly, "maybe you could find a spare jacket among your kids' things."

“That’s not the point,” the woman named Lexie said.

“What is the point?”

Her sister leaned over. “The point is,” she said in a low voice, “Lexie dated Will for a little bit one summer, way back when we were in high school, and he dumped her.”

“Sheila!”

Was there anyone Will *hadn’t* dated?

Then Lexie cleared her throat and nodded in the direction behind Allie.

Allie glanced back. Will was coming toward her. “Hey, I’m going to take Eli home,” he said. “He’s not feeling well.”

“No wonder, when he’s dressed wrong for the weather,” Lexie said.

Will looked puzzled. “He is?”

“Yes, it’s too cold for shorts and no jacket,” Sheila said.

Will still looked blank. He focused on Allie. “Anyway, we’re going to take off. Do you want to ride with us or get another ride?”

The two women were both looking at her, as was Will. And, she noticed, Stone was eyeing her too.

Allie felt disgruntled with everyone: Will, Stone, and the two snotty women.

"Sure, I'll ride with you," she said. "And I'm sure we can find some warmer clothes if you think Eli needs them. Up to you, though. You're a perfectly good father."

Stone's expression grew puzzled. Clearly, he wasn't following the subtext.

Allie was glad. She was ashamed of how suspicious and nosey her fellow church members—and her brother—were acting.

As Will, Allie, and Eli walked off together, Allie saw questions in Will's eyes. What was she going to say to him?

Lexie had been acting snotty, and okay, it was understandable if Will had dated and then dumped her. But wasn't there a more adult way to work that out than making snippy comments about Will's parenting? About his child's fashion choices, for Pete's sake?

Stone was unduly suspicious, and the women in the singles group had asked too many intrusive questions.

She shouldn't have let all of it upset her. She should have just gone ahead and smiled and let them all work it out themselves. After all, they were at a church picnic. All of them should have acted better. She should have kept her cool.

Except it was hard to do. She knew what it was like to have people gossip about her. She'd had plenty of that when she'd been involved with another teacher in her district who'd ended up being a liar. She remembered all too well the alienated feeling as everyone had whispered about her. She wanted to defend Will.

But Will! He was a mess, running hot and cold on her all the time.

Well, she was getting a ride home with him, and then she was going right into her own house and watching some junky show on TV. She was going to forget all about handsome Will and his cute son and their mutual neediness. She was going to take care of herself.

14

None of it would have happened if Eli hadn't started to cry.

Will was driving home from the church. From church, which he'd actually found tolerable. He hadn't grown up attending, and on the few occasions he'd gone to church as an adult, he'd found the program boring and the people a little too righteous for comfort.

At the same time, after everything had gone south so badly overseas, he'd ended up talking to a chaplain who had basically saved him. Talked him out of ending his own life, insisted that Will could still do good in the world. The man had shared verses and chapters from the Bible that had shored up Will when he'd been as low as dirt. In the end, Will had prayed the sinner's prayer.

So officially, he was a Christian. But he wasn't a very good one, especially in terms of attending Sunday services. Except now there was Eli to consider. He didn't want Eli to grow up in the rootless, faithless way Will had. He wanted to give the boy a spiritual grounding and a church community. Like in so many other areas of life, becoming a father had instantly changed everything. Mostly, it had gotten Will to look past his selfishness and his boredom and had forced him to see the bigger picture.

Today, he had to admit, the church people had been pretty nice, at least most of them.

Allie hadn't been any too friendly, but he'd heard her defend him. Now, though, she was cool and distant, and he didn't like it.

At the same time, it was necessary. He couldn't be with her. He'd had to pull away.

Maybe he should talk to her about why.

Afternoon sun was casting a golden light on the fields as he drove to the farm. When the silence in the truck felt oppressive, he tried to make small talk. “Ready for school tomorrow, Eli?” he asked.

There was a sound from the back seat, an odd sound. Will looked in the rearview mirror.

Eli was screwing up his face in preparation for a big… something. A cheer? A tantrum?

“I don’t want to go to school!” Eli kicked the back of Will’s seat, hard, over and over.

“Stop it.” Will slowed down. “What’s the matter?”

“I don’t wanna go!” Eli was yelling now. “I want Mommy.”

“I thought you liked school, honey,” Allie said over Eli’s cries. “Remember how much fun you had last week?”

“I want to stay home with Gus!” Eli’s voice was ear-splitting.

Will was grateful that they were almost back to the farm. He pulled into the driveway and stopped the truck. He climbed out and sucked in a breath, welcoming the break from Eli’s screams.

Then he opened the back seat. “Stop crying and come on,” he said, a command Eli ignored.

Allie had climbed out too, and now she was standing beside Will. "Do you want me to try to settle him down a little?"

"I would be incredibly grateful," he said.

She reached into the truck, unfastened Eli, and held him, face out, probably in an effort to avoid those kicking legs and thrashing arms. She sank onto the edge of the driver's seat and cuddled Eli, rocking him back and forth.

Eli's cries slowed down. Will could only admire Allie's beauty and her ability to nurture, her knowledge about kids.

Then he thought of a way to help settle his son. He jogged to the house and let Gus out. The dachshund sniffed around for a minute and then seemed to hear Eli. He ran to the boy, his short legs pumping. Will followed.

"Look, honey, there's Gus," Allie said quietly.

Eli slid out of her arms and onto the ground and put his arms around the dachshund. Gus licked his face with every appearance of concern.

Will took a step back, and Allie stood beside him, both of them watching the boy and dog.

"All the face licking doesn't seem too sanitary," Will said.

"But if Gus can make him feel better, it's worth it," Allie said.

It seemed to be working. Gus struggled out of Eli's arms and went into a play bow, barking, tail wagging. And Eli smiled.

Relief. Will looked over at Allie, meeting her eyes. "Thank you for settling him," he said, "I've been wanting to talk to you. If you have time, come in, I'll make a fire and we can roast some marshmallows. And talk after Eli goes to bed."

"Marshmallows?" Eli looked up, his upset apparently forgotten.

Good. In the midst of all his mistakes, Will had done two things right: he'd gotten the ingredients for s'mores, and he'd gotten a stack of picture books from the library. It was an evening's entertainment for a five-year-old, whether Allie was willing to participate or not.

But he hoped she would.

"S'mores and a story with Gus in front of the fire, and then to bed," he said to Eli. It would be an early bedtime, but given the meltdown, that was probably just what Eli needed.

"Okay!" Eli sat up straighter and ran to find a stick to throw for Gus.

"Don't feel obligated," Will said to Allie. "You've already done so much for me."

He meant it, but still, he felt breathless watching her think about it, waiting for her decision.

The cool air lifted strands of her hair and blew them across her face. She brushed them back and tucked them behind her ear. Then she smiled, and Will felt like the sun had just come out after a storm. "How can I turn down s'mores?"

Forty-five minutes later, Eli was bathed and in his pajamas, and Will had built a fire. There was a tap on the door, and then Allie walked in, dressed in sweats and a crewneck shirt, thick socks, and sandals.

She was completely covered from head to toe, and Will had never seen anyone more appealing.

They found old-fashioned wire hangers they could use for roasting marshmallows and showed Eli how to hold one over the flames. Allie ended up dropping her marshmallow into the fire, and she stuck out her lower lip and pouted, making Eli and Will laugh.

Gus sat up on his back legs, begging, his long body quivering and wavering.

"Can I give him a marshmallow, Daddy?" Eli asked.

The word *Daddy* melted Will's heart. "I don't think marshmallows are good for him, but you can get him a couple of dog treats."

Eli ran to the kitchen and brought back some small dog treats, then made Gus shake hands and roll over.

Will was impressed. He hadn't even realized the dog could perform like that.

They put together s'mores, and Eli took a big bite. "Mom made these once," he said through a mouthful of chocolate and marshmallow.

Will's heart squeezed. Eli's mother had made him s'mores. She must've helped him teach the dog tricks.

She hadn't been a bad mother. Will could see that. He really wanted to know what had happened. Really hoped that she could be involved in Eli's life in some way.

After they'd eaten their fill of s'mores, Allie started looking through the stack of picture books. "Want me to read while you cuddle up?" she asked.

Will would've thought to do it the other way, to let Eli cuddle up with Allie. She was the nurturing one. But she was probably right. Eli needed to learn that Will could comfort him too.

After a couple of picture books, Eli nodded off. Will carried him upstairs, asking Allie to wait. When he came back down, he paused on the stairs just to look at her in the firelight.

She was so young, her face so fresh and innocent with its sprinkle of freckles across the nose. Her shiny hair, her sparkling eyes... Will's throat went dry.

He needed to remember his goal. He wanted to talk things through with Allie, to explain to her why he'd gotten cold, why he'd backed off, why he couldn't be with her.

He settled himself beside her, both of them leaning against the couch, looking into the fire. "Look, I hate to use the old line, 'it's not you, it's me,' but it's the truth. I'm messed up from my time overseas. I made a big mistake, and, well, it's made me even worse at relationships than I used to be."

She nodded, not looking at him, staring into the fire. After a moment, she spoke. "Mistakes in wartime are just so serious. Makes me glad the worst thing I could do is upset a child for a little bit of time."

"Yeah," Will said. "That's why I'm in the line of work that I'm in now, restoring old farm equipment. Can't hurt anyone doing that."

"I'm sorry that happened to you," she said. She put a soft hand over his and squeezed.

Marvel of marvels. Allie didn't seem to hate him. She sympathized.

"I just don't want to hurt anyone else," he said. "That's why I'm steering clear of relationships." That and the fact that he didn't deserve happiness after what had happened.

"Did you ever think that maybe you'd help others, not hurt them?"

"Not really," he said.

"You're already doing it," she said. "You help people by restoring their old farm equipment. You're helping Eli. You're being a good dad."

That made him laugh a little. "Yeah, thanks for defending me at the church picnic," he said. "I have so much to learn. I didn't even think of putting a jacket on Eli."

"But you're trying," she said. "That's all any of us can do."

He turned his hand over to grip hers. It felt warm. Soft. Delicate. "You're so kind. So pretty. If I could be with anyone, if I could pursue anyone, it would be you."

She looked as if she wanted to say something. Started to, then stopped.

Then, slowly, she rose to her knees, leaned toward him, and kissed him.

Her lips on his tasted like the finest wine, felt like soft cashmere.

There was no way he could turn away. Instead, he wrapped his arms around her and deepened the kiss.

15

As Will wrapped his arms around her and kissed her more deeply, Allie felt like she was floating in a warm, comforting sea. Except... if it were warm and comforting, why was her heart pounding so hard?

Will's hands were gentle, stroking her hair, and his strong arms offered the protection she'd always wanted and rarely experienced. She buried her face in his neck and inhaled his clean, spicy scent.

She felt shaken by it, but also, in an odd way, safe. She could tell from his tender touch that Will wasn't going to push her further than she wanted to go.

They were both breathing hard by the time he pulled away. Will held her hand for a moment, looking into her eyes as if he wanted to memorize them. Then he dropped her hand and turned away. He walked over to the dark window and looked out, even though the darkness had to prevent him from seeing much, if anything.

Finally, he spoke. "I'm sorry, Allie."

She still felt dizzy, swept away, exhilarated. "Why are you sorry? It was my idea."

He turned back. "You should probably go home while you can," he said, softening the dismissal with a crooked smile.

"Do I have to?" she teased. She knew she'd end up going home. No way could she spend the night, even on his couch, after that kiss. But she wanted to let him know that the idea appealed to her.

His expression went serious. "Yeah, Allie. You do."

She didn't know what his expression meant. She felt too overwhelmed and excited to figure it out. So after looking at him for a moment longer, she turned and hurried to her tiny house.

All night, Allie thought of Will, half

awake, half dreaming. It was a warm, exciting, comforting feeling, something she'd never felt before. She cared for Will more than she'd ever cared for anyone.

She got up and had her breakfast early. When she saw out the window that Will and Eli were headed for the bus stop, she couldn't resist. She threw on a jacket and hurried outside to walk with them. She had done it several times before, especially when she was staying over at his place. Today, she couldn't have stayed away if she tried.

He smiled at her, and Eli reached out a hand. So she, Will, and Eli walked to wait for the bus. It came all too quickly, and Eli climbed on, so cute with his big backpack.

They waved to the bus and then turned and walked back toward the farmhouse and her tiny house.

Will cleared his throat. "Uh, Allie. I was planning to talk to you today. Now's as good a time as ever."

Her stomach twisted. "Talk about what?"

"I don't think we should do this."

"Do what?"

"Well, for one, I don't think we should walk Eli to the bus stop together. It's giving him expectations. Plus, the kids see it and the bus driver sees it, and they're making it into something that can't be."

Her steps slowing, she looked at Will. He'd told her from the beginning that he wasn't up for a relationship. He'd pulled away from her last night, after kissing her. For that matter, she herself wanted to stay single. She'd committed to that, and for good reason, given her history.

And yet… her own feelings for him were enough to consider changing her mind. And she could have sworn he felt something for her, too. Something strong. Or at least, something to explore. "Are you sure it—us—is something that can't be?"

He stopped, turned, and faced her. "I'm sure, Allie. It can't."

His eyes were sad but certain, and she couldn't look into them for long because it hurt too much. She reached out for him, couldn't help it.

He took her hand in his larger, calloused one. And then he put her hand away, back by her side. "It can't be, Allie," he said. He turned and walked toward the farmhouse.

Allie stared after him, tears springing to

her eyes, her throat tightening. Afraid she was going to cry where he, or someone else, would see, she speed-walked to her door and let herself inside the tiny house. She climbed to the loft and threw herself down on the bed.

She was an idiot. She had known Will didn't want a relationship from the get-go.

But here she was, getting her hopes up. Initiating a kiss. Acting like she was lovable.

She wasn't lovable, not in that way. Sure, kindergarten kids loved her, but age-appropriate men? Nope.

This was just more evidence of what she'd already known.

For a little while, she gave in to stormy tears. She wanted Will. She wanted Will and Eli, all they'd shared together. She didn't want to be alone again, grieving the loss of something that had never been what she'd thought it was.

Then she forced herself to sit up, wipe her face, take deep breaths.

She wasn't going to let this stop her. She was going to get back to where she had been even a few days ago: strong and independent.

She looked out the window. Will was

walking toward the barn where he did his work. His shoulders were slumped, his steps uncharacteristically slow. Sadness tugged at her, sadness for a man who couldn't let anyone close.

Couldn't, or wouldn't? He hadn't even tried.

No. She wasn't going to stay on the same property as him, couldn't bear it. She gathered her laptop and purse and headed down to Abbott Farm.

The first person she saw when she got out of the car was Jenn.

"Hey, hon," Jenn said. "Working over here today?"

Allie steadied herself with a deep breath. "Yep."

Jenn tilted her head and studied her. "How's everything going?"

"Fine," Allie said. As long as she limited herself to one-word answers, she could hold it together.

"Really? You don't look so good."

To Allie's horror, tears rose to her eyes again, and she couldn't speak for the tightness in her throat.

Jenn took her hand and pulled her toward her home, right next door to Abbott Farm. "Tell me what happened," she said, shoving a plate of coffee cake Allie's way and dropping teabags into cups.

Before the kettle had boiled, Allie had started telling Jenn everything that happened—their attraction, their kiss, and his withdrawal.

Jenn poured water into their cups. "Do you think it was because Stone lectured him?"

"No. Not really. He has things in his past that have put him off love. He was clear about that. It's my fault we veered in that direction, not his. And I need to forget about him. Like some wise person said, when they tell you who they are, listen."

David tapped on the screen door and came inside. He raised an eyebrow. "Am I interrupting something?"

"Yes, but it's okay," Allie said.

Jenn put a hand on her shoulder. "You sure? We can talk more."

"No. I want to get a lot done today."

"That's what I came to ask about," David said. "What's the holdup? Let's get a group of kids to walk through. We'll get Paisley and

Maddie to do it, and maybe we can ask Eli to join in, too."

"No," Allie said, too sharply.

David tilted his head and studied her. "Why not?"

"I don't want to ask him." Allie looked away from David's insightful gaze.

He came over and sat down beside her. "What's wrong?"

What *wasn't* wrong? Allie's insides were mush, like she'd been run through the old wringer washer that sat as a decoration on Pop Abbott's front porch. "I can't talk about it. I'm going to go work at the farmhouse."

As she headed out, David called to her, "Okay if I ask Will?"

She just wanted to get rid of her interfering siblings. "Sure. No. I don't know." She walked away quickly.

Hopefully, Jenn would tell David not to invite Will and Eli to anything for a little while. But of course, that couldn't last. Will was a neighbor and friend. Plus, Allie lived on his farm. There was no way she could avoid him.

She'd have to toughen up, or she'd have to leave.

16

It was Friday afternoon, and Will was glad of it.

He hadn't been sleeping well all week. Not since kissing Allie and then pushing her away.

He stood at the bus stop on the rural road in front of the farm, waiting for the bus that would bring Eli home from school. He'd thought to bring a big umbrella, but no jacket for himself, and he was shivering in his lightweight T-shirt.

Had Eli worn a warm jacket to school? Will didn't remember. He was amazed at all the details that went into raising a young child. Hopefully, if he *hadn't* dressed Eli warmly enough, someone had lent him a sweater.

He glanced back toward the tiny house. He knew that Allie was in there, because he'd heard her car pull up about an hour ago.

Hearing it made his heart jump, made hope rise in him that she would come over, be friendly, act like they were cooperating with one another as they had before.

But they'd kissed, and that had changed everything.

He couldn't be kissing Allie. He didn't want to hurt her like he had hurt women and children in the past. In particular, one child. His mind skittered away from Imad and his mother. He'd fallen short, hadn't managed to save them, and he would always regret that, would always blame himself. But he had the chance to try again with Eli, and although he didn't feel adequate for the task, there was comfort in knowing that he didn't have a choice. He had to rise to the occasion. Had to do a good job, because there was no one else.

Women? That was a different issue. He'd hurt more than one woman, and in different ways. He'd hurt women with his thoughtless dating, his love-them-and-leave-them style. He'd also hurt Imad's mother by not protecting her and her child.

He'd been right when he'd promised himself he wouldn't get involved with women anymore. His plan to stick to himself, focus on his craft, his career that he loved, was a good one. At least, it had seemed to be.

What he hadn't anticipated was that Eli would burst into his life, removing the option of being a solitary hermit. Already, he'd met several other parents and kids when he'd taken Eli to the park to play. And through Allie, he and Eli had met more of the crew at Abbott Farm.

No, solitude was no longer an option.

He could protect Allie, though. He could protect her from himself, avoid hurting her by backing out of whatever it was that had started to spark between them.

Although he had actually hurt her by pushing her away, his heart reminded him.

The yellow school bus chugged through the rain, and Will stood by the open door to hold the umbrella over Eli. The kiddo walked off the bus like he'd been doing it all his life, his backpack on his back. He was such a trooper. Such a brave kid.

Today, he looked a little tired. It was still a long week for him, little guy that he was. Allie had mentioned—before they'd gotten estranged—that kindergarten was a big adjustment for kids, especially those used to staying at home rather than being in a group environment. From things Eli had said, Will had deduced that his mother had indeed kept him at home, although he'd attended preschool a couple of mornings a week.

So Eli had to adjust to being out in the world, behaving appropriately every day. It was a lot for a kid. Not only that, but Eli was still adjusting to life with Will rather than his mother.

As they walked back toward the farmhouse, Will asked Eli about his day.

"Did you do anything fun at recess?" he asked.

"No." Eli scowled. "Recess was inside."

"Any fun art?"

"No." Eli pointed at the tiny house. "Can we go see Miss Allie?"

"Not now," Will said.

"But she's in there. I know she's in there. See, her light is on."

"Yes, but she's probably busy working." Taller than Eli, Will could see that Allie was hunched over her kitchen table, poking away at her laptop.

If Will hadn't kissed her, he could pop over, let Eli say hi, ask her if she needed a break. They could be friends.

But the kiss had ruined everything.

Eli was still staring toward Allie's house.

"Come on," Will said. "Gus has been waiting for you."

"Gus!" Eli said, distracted for the moment.

They went inside, and it was true, the little dachshund was ecstatic to see Eli, who dropped to the floor and let the dog lick his face and hands.

Will got Eli a snack—graham crackers and milk—and then settled him on the floor with his race car set, a TV show on in the background. Will needed to do some bookkeeping for his business, so he sat at the dining room table where he could keep an ear out for any needs that Eli had.

The business was doing well, and he was

starting to get a lot of commissions for Christmas. He was going to have to close down on that, or else hire someone to help him, which he wasn't really prepared to do at this point. He liked working alone, being a one-man shop. Liked being able to guarantee that quality work would be done.

Being too popular was a good problem to have.

He spent some time juggling with his calendar to see how much more work he could afford to bring in, how much he could do before Christmas.

He heard the front door open and then close.

Immediately, he stood. "Eli? You there?"

"Yeah," Eli said.

Will's elevated heart rate settled. "You know you can't go outside without me."

"I didn't," Eli said. He flopped back down and went back to making race car noises in the living room.

Will guessed the child was peopled out after a week of school. That was the only way to explain him playing by himself, contentedly, rather than fussing for Will to entertain him.

Half an hour later, Will figured he'd done enough and went into the living room, where Eli was looking out the window. Rain ran down it in streaks.

"Not so nice out," he said. Hesitantly, he put a hand on Eli's shoulder. He still wasn't sure how much physical affection to show his son, wasn't clear on how to do it. His instincts around children were pretty muted, but he was trying to follow them, such as they were.

Eli leaned against him. "Gus will find her," he said confidently.

"Find who?" Will looked down at his son, puzzled.

"Miss Allie," he said. "I sent Gus out to find Miss Allie."

"What? You let Gus outside?" Will looked around the room and, seeing no sign of the dachshund, rushed to the door and looked out. Rain was coming down in buckets, and even though it was only five o'clock, it seemed to be getting dark.

There was no sign of the little dog. "You just sent Gus out into the rain?"

Eli nodded, edging against the wall,

looking scared. "I wanted Miss Allie. I'm not 'llowed to go out by myself, but Gus is."

It was true, Gus went outside to do his business on his own, but Will usually kept an eye on him. "That was a dangerous thing to do, with nobody watching," Will said, only belatedly realizing that it had come out too loud, almost as a yell. But he was fond of the grouchy little dog and didn't want harm to come to him.

Eli started crying.

Great. Will knelt in front of him. "Hey, it's okay," he said. "But we have to work hard to find Gus."

He stood quickly, helped Eli get into a raincoat and boots, and shrugged into his own parka. They headed outside, hunting and calling for the dog. "You stay close to me," Will ordered. The last thing he needed was for Eli to get lost, too.

There was lightning in the distance, followed by a boom of thunder. Eli grabbed Will's hand. When the lightning and thunder got closer, Will ended up carrying Eli. They shouted for the little dog, looked in all directions, but there was no sign of him. It didn't help that Gus was black and didn't show up too well against the twilight.

Will didn't want to do it, but they ended up at Allie's door. Will set Eli down and knocked, and Eli yelled.

Allie opened the door, and—oh, blessed sight—Gus was in her arms.

"He found you!" Eli said.

"He did," she said, smiling at Eli. Not at Will, though.

A heap of muddy towels lay on Allie's floor. Gus must've come in dirty.

"I'm sorry he brought in dirt with him, but I'm relieved to find him. We were worried he was lost."

"I texted you that Gus was here," she said.

Will slapped his back pocket and realized that his phone was back at the house, charging, the sound turned off.

Eli clung to Allie's leg, and she knelt and cuddled him in one arm, letting Gus down to run circles around them, barking.

"I missed you," Eli said, hugging Allie.

"I missed you too, honey," Allie said. Her dark head bent over Eli, and she pulled him into her lap. She was so pretty and so nurturing. It would've been great for Eli if Will could have made this work.

Unfortunately, Will's own limitations meant that Eli would never have a mother. If things had been different, Allie would have made a great mother for Eli.

After a few minutes of cuddles and quiet talk, Eli started rolling around on the floor with Gus.

That left Will and Allie to stand together awkwardly, watching them.

Since she didn't start a conversation, Will cast around for something to say. "I really am sorry to bother you," he said.

She gave him a look, mouth twisted down, one eyebrow raised. "It's not me who needs distance."

"I'm sorry," he said. "I wish things were different."

Their eyes met, held. He hoped she could read the sincerity in his eyes. It was killing him to stand here and not reach for her.

"You're really sticking with this decision to stay away from me?" she said.

"For your own good," he said.

"Yeah, right." Her voice was bitter.

She crossed her arms tight over her

chest, and he felt horrible that he was the one who had caused her this pain. He was the one who had hurt her.

He was honored, truly honored, that she seemed to still want to be with him. It wouldn't last, of course. She'd find someone else, someone better, someone who wouldn't hurt her.

"I'm sorry," he said again, feeling the lack in that. Although he was apologetic, there was no way he would change his mind. Allie was better off without him. He enticed Eli with promises of Marshmallow Crunch cereal for dinner, and he, Eli, and Gus headed back to the farmhouse.

17

Monday morning was sunny, crisp, smelling of apples and leaves. A beautiful fall day on Abbott Farm.

But Allie wasn't smiling. No, she was annoyed, pretty much with everyone.

Her primary issue was with the Flock. Stone, Jenn, and David had just assumed that she would be glad to cover a visit from a local senior center. She'd learned about it Friday night, just after that miserable encounter with Will, Eli, and Gus. She'd argued that she wasn't knowledgeable about working with seniors, but her siblings had also claimed ignorance, and they said that she would do just fine.

So she'd spent the weekend researching and planning the visit. Now, she was at the farm early, consulting her tablet and making sure that access and signage were clear, and reviewing the program she intended the visitors to follow.

She made sure the restrooms were clean and accessible—that was always priority number one—then walked through the barn, checking for obstacles and dangers.

When she emerged, David strode over to her. "Hey, thanks for doing this," he said. "You needed a practice run, right?"

"I needed a practice run with *kids,*" she said.

"This will be similar, won't it?"

Allie rolled her eyes. "Not hardly. And it's taking away from time I need to put the kids' program together."

David pinned her with a sharp gaze. "Look, since you're not bringing in money yet with your school-visit program, this will be a good way for you to contribute. They're paying for the visit, and if we do well with it, we may be able to invite other senior groups to visit."

"I'll do it this time," she said. "But I don't want to be the only one who's managing all the community visits for the farm."

"Oh, of course," he said, but he was checking his messages on his watch, not paying a whole lot of attention.

"You'll be here to help today, right?" she asked him.

He glanced up from his messages on his smartwatch. "Sure, probably," he said. "But you won't be alone. Will's participating in this visit."

"What?" Shock waves almost knocked Allie to the ground. She stared at David, disbelieving.

"It'll be fine, Allie. Just work with him. The seniors want to see his restoration work, but they didn't want to go to two different farms. And anyway, Will's not set up for visits like we are, with restrooms, parking, stuff like that." He glanced again at his watch. "Uh-oh. Courtney needs me down at the farm stand. I have to go. You and Will can handle this, right? Send them down after and we'll sell a ton. It'll be great. Thanks, sis."

And he was gone.

Allie growled to herself. She was working with Will, then. How did it always come to that? At first, it hadn't been bad, but now he'd actively dumped her once, then reiterated the dumping when Gus, the dachshund, had scratched at her door and come to visit.

Oh, she knew he hadn't really dumped her, because they hadn't actually been dating. But it had sure felt like being dumped to Allie.

When Gus landed at her tiny house, Allie had actually thought it might lead to her reconnecting with Will. The more fool her.

She thought of Eli's joy when he'd seen his missing dog. What a sweet child. He was what she missed most about not seeing Will, she told herself firmly.

He wouldn't be here today, though. He was in school.

Allie walked through the route she'd planned for the visit. They didn't have animals, aside from the two dairy cows. They'd add chickens at some point. But for now, this was a crop farm, and the seniors would probably like seeing Stone working on the vegetable harvest. He had a giant field cultivated with corn and tomatoes and kale, and everything was ripe and gorgeous now. Stone looked like a modern-day farmer hero as he worked his way down the rows, examining each individual vegetable. So that would be a good part of the visit.

And who didn't like flowers? Jenn had mums and asters now, as well as some goldenrods. Allie walked over to the flower field, and Jenn came to greet her at the fence. She was the only one who was somewhat sympathetic to Allie's point of view.

"Are you going to manage this visit okay?" she asked. "I know it was dumped on you. I can bring in a couple of buckets of flowers and they can take home bouquets. Do you think that will be a good addition to whatever you've planned?"

"Sure," she said. She didn't pretend enthusiasm, and Jenn looked crestfallen.

"Thanks," Allie said. "Really. It's just... I found out Will is going to be involved in this visit, with his restored equipment. I'm really not in a mental space to work with him."

"Uh-oh. I didn't realize." Jenn squeezed her arm. "We'll talk later," she promised.

"Can you do it with me?" Allie asked, as she watched Will's truck pull into the parking area.

"Can't," Jenn said, sounding regretful. "I have a video call with a vendor." She headed toward the house.

Allie sucked in a breath, sighed it out, and walked over to where Will was climbing out of his truck.

Of course, he looked gorgeous. His hair still a little wet from the shower, his T-shirt clinging attractively to his broad chest and strong arms. His jeans, old and low-slung and very, very flattering.

She smacked herself mentally. "I wish you'd let me know you were involved," she said as she approached him.

His eyes met hers, and then he looked away. "I just found out last night," he said. "I thought they were going to do a quick stop by at our farm, but then David let me know that it all needed to take place here. I gotta get this stuff unloaded."

He went to the back of the truck and

started pulling boxes and carts of equipment out. "Where do you want me to set up the display?"

Well, since I had no idea you were coming... "How about over here at this edge of the parking area? That way, we can have your part be last, and you'll have a little more time to set up."

"Thanks," he said. He started pulling and tugging at a tarnished metal item that looked like a bicycle, with a bucket where the seat should have been.

She took one end of it and helped him lift it to the ground. "Now, hand me those rakes and pitchforks."

He handed them down, and they worked quietly together for a few minutes, roughing out an area for him to use, setting up a makeshift workbench.

"Thanks for helping, Allie," Will said when his truck was unloaded, flashing her a hesitant smile. "I mean it."

She was spared answering him by the arrival of two short buses. They chugged in, and she gestured to where they should park, which made her realize they needed a director of traffic when the buses first arrived. Lesson number one.

She took a couple of deep breaths, trying to settle her heart rate after the unexpected time spent close to Will. She needed to get through this obligation, this visit, with grace. She needed to learn from it and help the family by doing it.

As the buses parked where she indicated, Pop Abbott came out of the farmhouse. He greeted people as they climbed off the bus.

He was serious about being and staying retired, and there was no obligation for him to work the farm. But any assistance he could provide would be welcome. Maybe he'd be willing to be the parking lot greeter. He was a sociable man and so pleasant to be around, plus he was a real farmer. He would make a wonderful first impression, whether on seniors or kids.

She helped people off the bus as needed, along with several workers from the senior center. As they made their way across the parking lot toward the vegetable area, she realized that there were a few problems with access for those with mobility issues. Several of their visitors used canes, two had walkers, and one was in a wheelchair, bundled up with a scarf and hat despite the warm weather. Allie recalled seeing the same woman outside the school one day when she and Will had picked up Eli. Must be a local grandma.

Allie wrote down *mobility* and *access.* That was likely to be a concern with some children in the classes that visited, too. The mainstreaming of children with disabilities meant that any group of students might include kids with mobility issues.

Everything was also going much slower than she expected—a real eye-opener. That would be the case with kids, too. It always took twice as long to get them to do what they were supposed to do.

Maybe her siblings had been right, she realized reluctantly. There were a fair number of similarities between visitors from schools and visitors from elder-care facilities.

As she walked with the visitors, she decided to be straight with them. "I'm so glad you're here," she said. And now that they were here, it was true. "I want you to know that I'm using you as guinea pigs, because I'm working on a program that will have school children visiting on field trips at the farm. So give me any feedback you have or ideas about what kids might like."

"Most of us are grandmas and grandpas," one man said. "We'll be glad to give advice. We're known for it!"

"Not necessarily loved for it, but known for it," someone else chimed in, and several people laughed, including Allie. Good. This was a happy, jovial group. Her mood was lifting already.

They reached the vegetable garden, and Allie hailed Stone. He was at the far end, harvesting kale. As they watched him approach with a bushel basket, the elders started talking about memories of their parents' and grandparents' victory gardens, topping one another with tales of being made to do onerous chores as kids.

Stone reached the fence, showed the guests what he'd been doing, and talked a little bit about the types of crops they could see. The sun was warm on Allie's back, and for the moment, everyone's attention was focused on Stone. Allie's shoulders relaxed a little more.

"You can buy produce afterward," he said as he finished his spiel, winking at Allie. As everyone turned toward the next event, he mouthed "thank you" to her, and she felt glad she was taking charge of the visit.

She led the group over to the flower field. Pop Abbott showed up with his big golf cart and gave a couple of the less mobile visitors a ride. Not a bad idea, she realized. She'd have to talk to Pop about either playing that role or finding someone who would.

The women in particular loved the flowers, which led to more talk and reminiscences. Jenn must still be on her video call, but Allie promised that everyone would get a little bunch of flowers at the end.

They reached the picnic area, and Allie passed out paper cups of apple cider and popcorn flavored with fresh rosemary from the farm. At this point, the guests had been here for over an hour and they seemed glad to sit down for a rest.

This was actually going well. The seniors were lovely.

"One more stop," she said after everyone

had enjoyed their snack break. "We're going to take a look at some antique equipment that Will Burton, from the farm just down the road, has been restoring."

She wasn't sure whether the women would enjoy that as much, but to her surprise, they seemed excited. Everyone nodded over the vintage wrenches, oddly shaped and tractor-specific, with embossed brand names. They raved over Will's cast-iron farm bells and the old pitchforks, reminiscing about how they had been used in the past, and discussing ways they would contribute to farmhouse décor now.

Will talked to them about the equipment, but mostly, he just asked if they had seen an item, and then listened to the stories. At one point, someone suggested that kids would enjoy demos with the old farm equipment, like the hand-cranked corn sheller, and Allie nodded. That was a good point. Although... was Will going to be involved in the school visits? More to discuss.

Allie didn't want to be enthusiastic about Will's display, but it did bring to mind that teachers might like to have history included in their lesson plans. Pop was still around, and he jumped in to talk with the visitors about old-time farming. Watching the group spend time together, chatting and laughing, Allie realized that this was living history.

Maybe some of these folks would like to be volunteer helpers when the kids came? She made another note.

Will continued to listen, prompt more memories, and discuss the old tools, talking about how he restored them. He was so gentle, so patient. He would be great with kids, just like he was great with these elders.

He wasn't making any effort to sell his services, but several people mentioned that they had items they wanted restored, so he got a clipboard out of his truck and passed it around so they could write their names and phone numbers on a list.

Watching him, Allie felt her heart warm in her chest. Oh, she didn't want this to happen, but she was falling for him again, seeing him in action.

Finally, she checked her watch and realized the group had been at the farm for two hours. Now it was time for them to get back on their buses and make a stop at the farm stand on their way out.

As they climbed aboard their buses, Jenn was there with flowers for all of them. Someone suggested that she might be able to do a flower arranging class at the senior center.

Their enthusiasm made Allie happy. Abbott Farm was really making a contribution to the community, and she loved it.

After the buses had pulled away, Jenn, Will, and Allie stood together. "Did you learn anything useful?" Jenn asked.

"I really did," Allie said. "Although I think they have a lot more patience than kids will have. We have to make sure to include a lot of hands-on elements for the kids. But," she went on, "it might be nice to do some combined groups, get the elders telling stories." Allie shared her idea of asking some of the seniors to volunteer.

Jenn nodded enthusiastically. "This has been a big success."

Pop Abbott came over in time to hear that, and he agreed, giving Allie a hug.

Allie's attitude had turned around. She was helping the farm, and she was getting ideas for her program. Working with Will hadn't been as bad as she feared. Although it had been painful to watch him, she also knew what a contribution he had made.

As they all started cleaning up, though, Will came over and touched her sleeve. "After we get done with this," he said, "can I take you to lunch so we can talk?"

18

As he pulled into a diagonal parking spot in front of the Bean Counter Café, Will wondered whether he was making a mistake, taking Allie to lunch.

But his goal was to become friends with her. Just friends, but real ones. He hadn't treated her well. He'd run away, and that didn't sit well with him. If they were to work together, be neighbors, they should be at least friendly.

And yeah, he was longing for more than friendship, but he wouldn't allow himself to go there. So his hope was that they could take a step today toward real, although platonic, friendship.

They walked inside, Will's hand hovering just an inch behind the small of Allie's back. *Don't touch her*, he reminded himself.

The smell of strong coffee and sweet cinnamon baked goods filled the air. The café had hardwood floors, blue-and-white curtains, and pleasant, upbeat music. It felt like a new place, although he was sure he'd come to this restaurant in years past. Must've been updated. It was nice.

Since it was lunchtime, they ordered sandwiches rather than pastries, and then Will broke down and got them a couple of big chocolate chip cookies to go with their coffee. Once their food was ready, they found a table among the many that were occupied. The place was buzzing, obviously popular.

They sat down and enjoyed their sandwiches for a couple of minutes. Will's was delicious, ham and cheese on a hard roll. Allie had gotten turkey and avocado, and her smile made his heart skip a beat.

After a few bites, Allie looked over at him. "You said you wanted to talk."

"I do," Will said. "I want to talk to you about being friends."

She raised an eyebrow. "You want that? Why, so we can work together?"

"Yeah. I guess that's the main reason." He paused, took a sip of coffee. "I'm sorry about how I pushed you away before. I kind of panicked, but there was no excuse for being so abrupt about it."

Two high spots of color rose in her cheeks. "It's not like I want to get married or anything," she said. "I'm committed to being single myself. I was just a little surprised at how quickly you backed way off."

He wanted to understand her. That was part of friendship, right? "If you don't mind me asking, what made you so committed to being single?" he asked.

She put down her sandwich and wiped her hands. "Just some stuff that happened in the past."

"Anything you'd feel comfortable sharing? With a friend?"

"Be careful what you ask for," she said, with a smile that looked a little bit forced. "I don't know if you know much about my background, but it's not that different from the rest of the Flock's. My parents couldn't deal with me, after a while, so my grandparents raised me until I was twelve."

A simple sentence, but Will read a world of pain in it. "What happened when you were twelve?"

She lifted her hands, palms up. "What can I say? I got mouthy, and my grandparents felt like they were too old to deal with me. That's when I landed in the foster care system."

"At Abbott Farm?"

"Not at first," she said. She tore off a piece of bread as if she was going to eat it, then put it down. "I lived with another family for three years. They had a lot of younger kids, and I helped take care of them. That's when I realized that working with kids was my jam."

"That's good," he said. "But... it didn't last?"

She shook her head. "No. They moved to another state and decided they had to cut down on the number of foster kids. I was the oldest, so they figured I was the most able to deal with, well, being dumped."

Will winced. "That stinks."

"It was pretty painful at the time," she said. "But I was lucky. My next placement was at Abbott Farm. It must have been a God thing, because it lasted. Pop Abbott and the Flock became my permanent family."

"That's great," he said. "But… is that why you went with being single? Have you always wanted to be single?"

She blew out a breath and crossed her arms over her chest. "No," she said. "I actually wanted to be in a relationship, but I didn't choose very well. I started dating a man at a school in my district last year. I felt like it was very promising, but then I found out he was actually married."

Will nearly jumped out of his chair. "What? He was married and concealed it from you?"

"Yep. Another teacher at his school finally told me. He shared what was going on with a few colleagues, and word got out. When I found out the truth… well, I guess I overreacted."

"I don't know if there's really an overreaction to that," he said. He could strangle the guy. How could someone do that to sweet, kind, beautiful Allie? "Is that why you left the district?" he asked.

"Well…" A little smile crossed her face. "I

kind of told a bunch of people about it. Which probably didn't do a lot for his reputation or his marriage. But professionally, nothing happened to him. And when it was time for new contracts, I found out that my job was cut. He was friends with the superintendent."

Will stared at her for a moment. Slowly, he shook his head. "Oh man, Allie, I'm sorry."

"Yeah, well, it kind of turned me off dating. I don't necessarily want to risk being in a relationship again." She looked at him, eyes narrowed. "Kissing you was a mistake. But the aftermath reminded me of why I want to stay single."

He winced again. "I'm sorry that what I did kind of piled on top of everything else that's happened to you."

A woman with long blonde hair, wearing a sundress, came over to them. "Remember me, Will?" she asked, and held out her hand, smiling.

He shook it. "I remember." And he did, but this was bad timing. She was one in a long line of women he'd spent time with when he'd stayed with his grandparents. He racked his brain for her name. "What are you up to these days?"

"I'm a social worker. Children and youth. Are you two together?" She moved her finger between Will and Allie.

"No," Allie said promptly. "We're just friends."

"Oh, great! I just wanted to say hi, since I really enjoyed dating you for that month or two, a few years back."

Allie's face was blandly interested.

Her name flashed into his mind at last. "Allie, this is Destiny. Destiny, Allie."

"Nice to meet you." Destiny turned back to Will. "I guess that older woman you left me for didn't work out?"

Will had a vague memory of trying to let Destiny down easy because he'd grown interested in a woman he'd met at a temporary job in town. His face felt hot. "A lot of what I did that summer didn't work out too well. I apologize if I was unkind to you."

"No worries." The woman shrugged. "I guess we were unkind to each other. Anyway, I'm single, so if you ever want to get together..." She let the sentence hang, smiling at him.

She was pretty, and seemed to have a sense of humor, didn't take herself too seriously. Will liked that. But he had no interest in dating her. "I don't date right now," he said. "But I wish you the best."

"Thanks," she said. "I guess." She gave Allie a rueful grin and turned away.

After she was out of earshot, Allie said, "See? Exhibit A of men."

"I'm not like that anymore," Will assured her.

"Okay, but why were you? Why are men like that? I really want to know."

Will forked his fingers through his hair. He was glad the coffee shop was emptying out a little bit. "For me," he said, "I was just emulating what I grew up with. Relationships don't last, and men are measured by how many women they can conquer."

"Conquer?" Allie's eyebrows shot up nearly into her hairline.

"My dad's word," he said, lifting his hands to ward off her annoyance. "Conquests, I guess he called them. I didn't enjoy being like that, not really. In fact, I'm ashamed. That's one bad thing about Orchard Springs. I sowed my wild oats here. It was the only permanent place in a military brat's life, and I wanted to come back because it feels like home. But the unfortunate thing is that everyone remembers me for how I used to be. I don't know if I'm going to be able to escape that reputation."

"You changed, huh?" She sounded skeptical.

Will looked at the table and then looked at her. "Like I mentioned before, I had an experience that changed me."

She studied him for a moment. "Do you want to talk about it? I mean, if we're going to be friends..."

Will broke off a piece of cookie and ate it while he thought about whether to tell her what had happened. He didn't talk about it much. Couldn't stand to. But maybe sharing a little bit of his story would help him heal. "There was a kid," he said. "He couldn't have been much older than Eli." Immediately, the image of Imad came into his mind. Sweat trickled down his back.

"Where was this?"

"Afghanistan," he said. "I was stationed there and got to know the country and community some. I was doing a routine check of an area when a kid I had befriended—his name was Imad—ran toward us."

Allie's eyes held compassion, but she didn't speak.

"The guy I was on duty with was a bit of a hothead. He raised his gun toward the kid. I was afraid he'd shoot, so I pushed it aside. I didn't want him to hurt a child."

She nodded, her forehead creasing. "Of course not."

"So the boy's mother, who I also knew a little bit—nice lady—came running toward us. She was saying 'no, no, no.' I'd helped her and her son learn a little bit of English."

He stared down at the floor, taking a deep breath, not sure if he could go on.

"And then Imad, this boy who I looked at as a sweet kid, pulled out a bomb."

Allie gasped. "A five year old had a bomb?"

"Five, six, yeah. It happened over there." He needed to finish the story before he broke down. "So my buddy aimed and shot him. But not before he threw the bomb at our vehicle. That blew up—big explosion—and my buddy was killed."

"Oh, Will." She put a hand over his and

squeezed briefly. "What happened to the boy's mother?"

"Shot by another US soldier. I was the only survivor of the incident."

She was holding his hand now. "I'm so sorry." After a moment, she added, "You have survivor's guilt, don't you?"

"Yeah. I do." That was what the chaplain had said.

He clung to her hand for a moment, focusing on the soft feel of it, focusing on her glossy brown hair and her pretty face, trying to keep himself in the moment rather than going back overseas in his head.

"It wasn't your fault, it doesn't sound like," Allie said.

He shook his head. "I should've been able to stop it. The look in that woman's eyes, her love for her son, the agony of watching him get shot… I'll never forget it."

"But he had a bomb," Allie said.

"He did. Some of the bad guys must've gotten to him, told him what to do, offered him money or food. Without his mother knowing. Or maybe she did know." His throat tightened too much to say more.

They sat there for a moment. There was

clatter of silverware around them and dishes, a few voices from tables across the room.

"So that's the experience that changed you?"

He nodded. "In all kinds of ways."

"Not womanizing anymore," she said.

"Yeah. Not even dating at all. I don't feel right going on with my life when she couldn't, when a kid was shot on my watch."

She frowned like she was going to argue, then shook her head. "I guess I get that. Did you get counseling?"

He nodded. "Yep. That's what saved me. And luckily enough, it was a Christian counselor. He helped me with my guilt and shame and showed me how Christ could heal. I don't know if anything but that—but Christ—would've been big enough to let me go on."

She looked puzzled. "But if you're healed by Christ..."

He shook his head. "I misspoke. I'm better, but I'm not healed, and I don't know if I ever will be. That's why I can only be friends. But Allie... I want to."

They met each other's eyes and something arced between them. It was a kind of attraction, but more of an emotional connection. The pain they experienced and shared seemed to bring them closer together in an emotional way.

Finally, she nodded. “But if we get attracted to each other, are you going to dump me again? Dump me as a friend, I mean?”

“We can’t let that happen. I want to try a friendship, a real friendship.”

“Well,” she said, brushing her hands together, “I guess we’ve both been through worse. Let’s give it a try.” She held out a hand in a businesslike way. He grinned and shook it and felt something electric pass from his hand to his heart. When she was being cute, she was *seriously* cute.

This wasn’t going to be easy, but he was pretty sure it would be worth it.

UNTITLED

The last Saturday in September was the community open house for Abbott Farm. Fortunately, the weather was crisp and sunny, a perfect fall day.

Will was glad for Allie, glad to be involved with this event that was part of the project that meant so much to her. He was glad about a lot of things, generally happy in the world.

Asking Allie to be friends had been the right move. Their talk had led to them hanging out with Eli, a few friendly chats, and a new level of ease between them. That comfortable friendship was what he wanted most.

Well, not *most*. He would have liked to be more than friends, but since that wasn't a possibility, then this warm, close feeling was the next best thing.

For today, he wanted to help Allie and be a friend to her. And he wanted to make more connections with people in this community, to continue building a life in this town for him and Eli.

Eli. He looked over at where his son was playing with another boy he knew from kindergarten. Will had intended to keep Eli with him while he manned the display of equipment at the event. But the other boy's mom had offered to watch him while Will worked the open house. It was good to see Eli running, happy, making friends.

Maybe the temporary alienation from Allie had been a good thing. At least, he didn't think it had hurt Eli. Instead, it had made Will and Eli closer. Not having Allie to run to, Eli had started depending more on Will. And Will had gained some confidence that he could handle scrapes and bruises and emotional upsets just as well as any other dad.

Will finished setting up his equipment in

the designated area and then lifted his face to the blue sky. Feeling the warmth of the sun, hearing the voices of friends and neighbors around him, he could believe that God cared and was on his side.

Even though it was just a few minutes after the event's ten o'clock start, people from the community were pouring in. Partly, of course, it was nosiness. Everyone wanted to see what was happening at Abbott Farm, to learn how Pop was doing, and whether the Flock had managed to bring the farm back as they'd hoped.

Part of it was people being supportive. Orchard Springs was a friendly, old fashioned place where community members helped one another. The locals wanted to show that they were together with Pop Abbott, and in favor of a local business doing well.

People came over to talk to him about his antique farm equipment right away, and he got into several conversations about various items, some of them reminiscences about using those elements in the past or having family members who had used them. Some people also wanted to talk about some old equipment they had in their barn, to ask if it was valuable in Will's eyes, to see if he might be able to work on it, get it back to looking and working well.

He hadn't anticipated it, but events like this were great for his business. He might actually consider hiring an assistant to help him pick up the pace of his restorations. He liked working alone, but he was starting to like connecting with others, too.

In between talking to people about antique farm equipment, Will watched Allie. She was in her element with the kids, guiding them around to several activity stations, checking on how everyone was doing, whether things were safe and accessible. She was also talking and laughing with her foster brothers and sister. The Flock was all here, at Allie's insistence, as was Pop Abbott. It was nice to see the family working together and supporting one another.

Several seniors from the visit last week approached him. They'd brought friends and were eager to show off what they'd learned from Will and what he was doing. Free publicity. Nice. There were a couple of people in wheelchairs, including the same bundled-up woman who'd visited with the seniors. This time, the ramps and other access features were clearly marked and easy to manage. Allie had learned from that first visit.

The morning sped by with lots of lively business. Will was surprised to look at his watch and see that it was almost lunchtime.

He was turning back toward his equipment when suddenly, a loud crack split the air.

The sound hit him like a physical blow, and he was running—running toward Eli, crashing him to the ground. "Get down, stay down!" he shouted. He wasn't letting his son be hurt or killed.

Dimly, he heard a few loud voices, questions. A flock of starlings settled back into the oak trees.

Next was Allie. He looked around for Allie. Where was she?

People were murmuring and looking around, but no one was down. No one was running or ducking.

"Ow, Daddy!" Eli was crying, holding his arm.

Will scanned the entire area, did a 360,

looking for danger. But there was none, apparently.

Just a lot of shocked-looking people staring at him.

Allie ran over and knelt beside the two of them. "Where does it hurt?" she asked Eli. Eli held out his arm, and she felt it from shoulder to wrist. "Does that hurt? That?"

Eli shook his head, tearfully, and pointed at a scrape on his elbow.

Allie nodded and gave the boy a gentle hug. "We'll get that washed off, honey, and it will feel better soon," she said.

Allie seemed to fade in and out, getting larger and smaller, wavy around the edges. Same with Eli. Will's surroundings seemed to morph back and forth from Middle Eastern desert to central Pennsylvania farm. Back and forth, back and forth. It made Will dizzy.

Allie put a hand on his shoulder. "I don't know what that noise was. Maybe it was a car backfiring. It wasn't a gunshot, Will, I don't think."

People had approached them now, some expressing concern for Eli, for Will, some just curious.

"Hey, Destiny," someone yelled. "There's a kid over here that's hurt."

The social worker he used to date, Destiny, pushed her way through the crowd and knelt beside Eli. "Everybody okay?"

"Did he hurt the child?" someone asked.

"The kid's fine," someone else said.

The voices seemed to echo in Will's head. He sat, shoulders slumped, as his adrenaline drained.

Someone was pulling Eli out of Will's grip. "I'll take him to get a bandage and some juice," Allie said, her voice soothing. "We'll come right back, Will. You talk to Destiny."

Will nodded. Allie was his friend. Allie would take care of his son.

Destiny was waving people away, and then she knelt beside Will. "Can you tell me what happened?"

"I heard a gunshot," he said. "Wanted to keep Eli safe."

"I heard that noise, too." Destiny's head tilted to one side. "But I don't think it was a gunshot. How could it be?"

"I know what a gunshot sounds like," he insisted. "I just wanted to make sure Eli was okay."

She nodded. "You landed on him pretty hard, according to a couple of witnesses," she said. "I'm concerned the boy may be in danger."

The boy may be in danger. The words echoed horribly in Will's brain, and the potential ramifications crashed in on him. "He's my son! I would never hurt him." Not purposely, anyway.

Allie pushed her way into their little circle. "Will's a veteran with PTSD," she explained to Destiny.

Destiny nodded. "Are you getting counseling?" she asked Will.

He shook his head. "Had some earlier. Not now."

She frowned. "It sounds like you may need to do that. There's a risk to your child if you're hallucinating or unable to control your physical reactions."

A risk to your child. He was a risk to his child.

Horror filled him. He'd done what he'd vowed not to do. He'd hurt a child.

Allie was talking to Destiny. "It's fine, he's a good man. This is something he's working on, working through."

The social worker said something inaudible.

"He's a veteran. We can't take his child away."

Will looked at Allie, her good heart shining in her face, and realized that if they remained together, even as friends, she would be defending him all the time.

And he wasn't worth it. He wouldn't do that to her.

"I'm wondering if temporary foster care might be the safest bet," Destiny was saying.

Will cringed.

Then a chorus of voices arose. Stone's was loudest. "Not foster care," he said.

"No way, that child can't go into foster care," Jenn added.

"That's right," David said. "He's much better off with his father."

They were defending him, trying to protect Eli from foster care. Will didn't know how to feel about that.

"Are any of you foster parents?" Destiny asked, looking around at the Flock.

Slowly they all shook their heads.

"If necessary, we can take Eli temporarily

while we research the situation," Destiny said.

She went on talking, but all Will heard was an echo of the words: take Eli. Take Eli.

He was still sitting on the ground, surrounded by a small group now, the Flock and Destiny. Allie was off to the side, holding Eli and watching everything unfold. The community event seemed to have come to a halt.

So he'd ruined Allie's event, too.

He had failed.

He pushed himself to his feet, murmured a few words of thanks to the Flock, and turned toward his farm. He didn't trust himself to drive, so he started walking. Walking back to his farm and his solitude.

The truth beat through his brain along with the sound of his footsteps.

He was going to lose his son. Social services was going to take him, and rightly so. Will couldn't argue that he was a fit parent, not after what he'd just done. So he'd make it easy for them.

He'd leave Eli before Eli was taken away from him.

19

With one arm around Eli, Allie watched Will stride away.

She wanted to run after him. She knew him well enough now to know that he must be terribly upset by what had happened, that it had probably hit him very hard. He would never have walked away from Eli unless he felt himself to be a danger to the child. It had been an accident, but he'd hurt and scared his son.

She couldn't run after him, though, because Eli needed her.

Somehow, she had to bring Will and Eli back together and be a friend to them, help them manage this situation.

"Where's Daddy going?" Eli asked.

"He had to go home for a while," Allie said. Her rule was never to lie to a child, but you couldn't explain a nuanced truth like Will's departure to a five-year-old.

People were crowding around them, including the social worker, but in between them, Allie noticed a woman in a wheelchair bumping over the grass toward them. The same woman who'd been bundled up in layers of shawls and blankets, only now, she'd shoved them aside. She wasn't a senior citizen at all. Forty at most.

Eli saw the woman, too, and his face lit up. He struggled away from Allie.

"Mom!" he yelled. He ran toward her.

Mom?

The woman was pale and looked unwell, and she winced when sturdy Eli landed on her lap. But she wrapped her arms around him, rocking him back and forth.

The woman in the wheelchair was Eli's mom?

Allie jogged over to the pair. "Hey," she said, keeping her voice calm. "Everybody okay?"

The woman glanced up, half-smiled and nodded, and then focused on Eli again.

"Anybody want to explain what's going on?" Destiny asked.

Allie looked over at her. "It's an unfolding situation," she said wryly. She looked at Eli, tapped him on the shoulder. "Hey, Eli. Is this your mom?"

The social worker was paying sharp attention.

"Yes, it's Mommy!" Eli bounced up and down on her lap. "Mommy, Mommy, Mommy!"

Wow. Each bounce was obviously painful to the woman, but the real pain was in her expression as she studied Eli and patted him. Of course she was in pain; she hadn't seen her son for weeks, if Allie was understanding the situation correctly.

Or rather, she'd seen him. Maybe even been watching him, if she was the woman Allie had seen one day at school pickup. But she hadn't interacted with Eli, and he hadn't seen her. No way could a five-year-old keep a mom sighting to himself.

She leaned forward and took Eli's hand. "Eli, honey, I think you should get off your mom's lap for a little bit. You're a very big, heavy boy."

"Such a big boy," his mother choked out through tears.

Eli laughed but obligingly climbed off his mother's lap.

The social worker took his hand. "Come talk to me for just a minute, and then you can come right back here," she said. She walked several paces away with Eli and began to talk to him seriously.

That left Allie with the woman in the wheelchair as Jenn and David herded the curious onlookers away. "You're Eli's mom? But how are you here? How..." She didn't even know what to ask.

The woman was terribly thin, that was apparent, even though she wore a heavy jacket and sweatpants. She had deep dark circles under her eyes.

Her letter had said she was sick. Clearly, she was very, very sick. But Allie didn't want to intrude by asking her what was wrong.

"I'm Athena Wells," the woman said finally. "A long-ago connection of Will's. As for how I'm here... I've been staying with a friend outside of town." She grimaced, and a hand went to her abdomen. "I wanted to stay away from Eli, but I haven't been able to resist checking up on him. While I still can." The last words were higher pitched, and she broke off and collected herself. She sucked in a breath. "I wasn't going to show myself, because I didn't want to confuse him. But after what happened today," she waved a hand toward the area where Will had knocked Eli over, "I couldn't risk having him go into the system."

"Good decision." It was Stone, standing behind Athena, nodding.

Jenn and David were thanking people for coming and ushering them out toward their cars. "Sorry about the family drama," Allie heard Jenn say to a couple of curious women who didn't seem to want to leave. "Everything's fine. We just have a few things to do here. Thanks for coming."

People were talking in hushed voices to one another and looking back, but they did head toward their cars.

Pop Abbott had been standing off to the side, observing, but now he walked over to Allie, Eli's mom, and Stone. "Why don't you all come inside," he said. "We can get you more comfortable and give you some space to reconnect with your son."

Allie blinked. Pop Abbott seemed to be taking all of this in stride. But maybe that figured. He was used to people's unusual family situations from his years of doing foster care with Ma Abbott.

"Thank you, I'd appreciate that." Athena hadn't taken her eyes off Eli, but now she looked from Stone to Allie to Pop. "You should know that it was a forty-ish man, a little overweight, balding, who fired that shot that upset Will. Not sure why he did it, but he came out from behind the barn looking satisfied with the chaos he'd caused."

Allie looked at Stone. "Ronald," they said in unison.

They headed toward Pop's house. Fortunately, one of the modifications that had recently been made to the farmhouse was a wheelchair ramp, so it was easy to get her inside and show her to the living room. Once there, Allie sat on a chair beside her. "Are you okay? Is there anything I can get you?"

Athena nodded gratefully. "I would love a cup of tea," she said. "I got myself pumped up on medicine for this event, but everything is wearing off and I'm probably going to crash soon."

So Allie brought out a cup of tea and some cookies, and they got her settled on the couch with an afghan over her lap and Eli at her side. Eli kept looking up at her and touching her arm, as if to make sure she was real.

Pop Abbott pulled Allie aside. "We'll take care of Eli and his mom for a little while. Give them some time together, but where we can keep an eye on them. You better go get Will and explain what happened. I don't think he saw Athena, and he'll need to be involved in any decisions that are made."

"Okay, I will." It was a good idea. In fact, it was what Allie wanted to do more than anything: to share this news with Will, to discuss it with him and get his take, get him over here and supervising Eli's reunion with Athena. She wanted Will and Eli to be happy together, and she wanted, if possible, to be a part of that, even if just as a family friend.

Fifteen minutes later, she was pounding on Will's door.

He didn't answer.

She rang the doorbell. "Will! I have to tell you what happened! Open the door!"

Inside, Gus was barking so loudly that she couldn't hear whether there were footsteps coming toward her. So she just kept knocking and yelling.

Finally, Will opened the door. His face was ravaged. She didn't know if he had been crying or having some kind of an attack or if this was an aftermath of the PTSD event that had happened earlier.

"I don't want to talk," he said.

"But it's about Eli," she said.

"That's why I'm pulling away," Will said heavily. "I'm a danger to him. You saw what happened."

"Yes, well, that needs to be worked out, but listen."

His face was closed.

"His mom came. He's over at Abbott Farm with his mom!"

That got his attention. Will's eyes widened.

"Her name is Athena Wells. Does that ring a bell?"

Will frowned. "Of course it does," he

said. "Athena was terrific." He looked puzzled. "But I thought..." He trailed off.

Obviously, there was a story there. But now wasn't the time to hear it. "Eli recognized her right away."

Will rubbed the back of his neck. "He's okay?"

"He's okay for now, but come back. He needs you both."

"No." Will shook his head. "I have to distance myself."

Allie's heart broke at the pain and self-loathing in his tone. "Please, do it for me," she begged. "At least let me tell you what happened. It was Ronald—"

He interrupted her. "For you, and for Eli, no." He closed the door firmly.

Allie sank down onto the porch steps and gave way to her tears. It was midafternoon, and the sun was shining now, warm on her legs. But Allie didn't feel warm.

She felt as if someone had kicked her in the stomach.

Will wouldn't even speak to her when there was such major news. Not only that, but he'd apparently made the decision to abandon Eli, the son he'd just started to connect with. Poor Eli. His little heart would be broken once again.

Clearly, Will was too troubled to be in a relationship with Allie. He couldn't even stay connected to his son. The truth left an aching, empty feeling in her chest.

She felt that familiar impulse to beg, to try to get him back. To make him realize he was responsible for Eli, even if he'd made a mistake. But she knew from experience that begging didn't work, either.

She'd been abandoned, and Eli had been abandoned, and she didn't know if she could stand it.

She squeezed her hands together and bowed her head and prayed. *Help, God, help.*

After a stretch of time—Allie couldn't tell how long—a car approached, and then footsteps came toward her. She lifted her head and saw Jenn. She wiped her face on her sleeve and sat up straighter. "Hey. Everything okay over at the farm?"

Jenn nodded. "Stone and Elena are hanging out with Eli and his mom. They brought their daughter over, and she told Eli how she didn't know she had a dad, and then found out Stone was her dad. So they're all kind of bonding over that. The weirdness of parents coming in and out of your life."

"How's Athena doing?"

Jenn shook her head. "Not well at all, physically. I don't know what her illness is, but it's serious. I'm guessing that's why she felt she couldn't mother Eli, but it's not my place to pry."

Allie gestured toward the door behind her. "It's Will's place to pry," she said. "But unfortunately, he hates himself too much. He thinks Eli will be better off without him." She met Jenn's eyes. "And me, too. He thinks I'll be better off without him, too."

"Oh, honey." Jenn hugged her. "You need to be with someone who has something to give. And Eli needs a father he can rely on. I know it hurts, though. I'm really sorry, Allie."

The sympathetic words brought more tears. "I really cared for him," Allie choked out. "And for Eli, too. But he doesn't want to try. We're not worth it to him.

Jenn held her while she ranted and cried. "Get it all out," she said soothingly, like she'd speak to a child.

So Allie did. She let herself feel all the things she normally held behind her cheery kindergarten-teacher façade. All the hurt she'd felt from her family leaving her, a hurt that was now being replayed between Will and Eli. The disastrous pain that had happened this past year, with the man she'd thought she'd loved, who'd turned out to be married.

And now, her own relationship with Will. "I thought maybe, just maybe, he was the one," she choked out. "That we'd build something together, something permanent."

"I could tell you were hoping for that," Jenn said as she pulled a packet of tissues from her bag and handed them to Allie. "He *is* a great guy in a lot of ways, but can he love you the way you deserve to be loved?"

"I don't know," Allie said slowly. She wiped her eyes and straightened her shoulders. "I can't ask him, or test him out, because right now he won't even talk to me."

"Allie, you deserve to be treated well," Jenn said. "The Flock loves you, you know that, right? And you're so pretty. Half the guys at church want to be introduced to you. You're going to end up in a relationship if you want one. If not, then you're going to be part of the Flock forever, and you're going to have a great life." She squeezed Allie's hand. "Let's pray."

So they did, and Jenn talked more to her about God's power and plan. "And we're going to take care of you," she promised. "All of us. You're not going to be alone in this."

Allie hugged her sister. "I don't deserve you."

"You *do* deserve me, and the Flock, and all the happiness in the world." Jenn patted her shoulder. "I've got to go back to the farm," she said. "But I know you'll figure out what's the right thing to do."

And ultimately, she already knew what to do. With God's help, she was going to resist and reject the narrative that said she was unlovable. She was lovable; she was a child of God. If Will couldn't appreciate that, or if he had too many problems to be in a relationship... Well, that was about him, not about her.

Slowly she stood and walked back toward her house. She was going to leave this one in God's hands. But she lifted her face and thanked Him for sending Jenn to remind her that she was fearfully and wonderfully made, and that she'd never be truly alone.

20

Will didn't sleep much that night. Instead, he spent it wrestling with himself, comforting Gus, and trying to talk to God.

Sending Allie away from the door had been hard. He heard the pain and anger in her voice and had wanted nothing more than to comfort her. But that would be unfair. He couldn't be a comfort to wonderful Allie, not long term. She needed to get over him.

Worse than sending Allie away was losing Eli. He couldn't even think about the empty bed in the room next door, the little boy who had to be wondering what was going on and where his new daddy was.

He hadn't known he was Eli's father for long. Just about a month. He hadn't been in the least prepared for parenthood. Eli had thrown a wrench into all his plans for a quiet, solitary life.

But God knew better than he did.

He and Eli needed each other. He needed to be in Eli's life, and Eli needed him.

The fact of Athena being Eli's mother was too strange to even think about.

When he woke up—or rather got up; he hadn't slept—one thing was clear: he needed to go to church.

He didn't exactly want to. He didn't want to face some of the same people who'd been at the event yesterday, when he'd made such an idiot of himself.

But he had to do something. If he didn't, he'd sink way, way down into despair, the kind you didn't recover from readily, if at all. He had to try to save himself from that, in case Eli needed him, in case there was something he could do—from a distance—for his son.

And he needed God's counsel in this complicated situation. Needed to know what God wanted him to do next. It wasn't going to come in a bolt of lightning, but in the quiet of church, he might get some insight. He had to try.

He let Gus out and stood in the cool, foggy morning air, watching the little dog run around, ears flopping. He breathed in the mix of leaves and hay and rich dirt that defined autumn.

He fed Gus and then spent a few minutes petting the little dachshund, who clearly missed Eli.

He didn't want to think about how much Eli must miss Gus.

All of that meant that he arrived at church late. He was standing outside the door, waiting for a prayer to finish, when he heard a creaking sound behind him. He turned and froze.

Could it be? Was it her?

Yes. Looking terribly unwell and unlike the vibrant woman with whom he'd had a brief romance, Athena, Eli's mother, was wheeling herself toward him.

She used a wheelchair?

He took two long steps to reach her. "Where's Eli? I heard you had him. Is he all right?"

"He's at Abbott Farm," she said. "He's safe with Pop Abbott and some of the Flock. He misses you, though."

She appeared calm, but he could tell from the set of her jaw that she must have steeled herself to confront him. He wanted to yell at her, to criticize how she'd managed everything, but she was so, so frail. Her arms, resting on the sides of her wheelchair, were like sticks. Her face was gaunt, and her hair, which had once been thick and beautiful, was thin, partially covered by a wide headband.

Unsure of where to start, he sat down on a bench to be at the same level as she was in her chair. "Why are you here? Did you follow me?"

"No. I did ask where I was likely to find you this morning, though. Plus, I needed some spiritual sustenance. But I can't go inside at church. Too easily infected." She held up a face mask.

He wanted to ask why, what was wrong with her, but he didn't want to be that rude.

"Do you remember that this is how we met, outside of church?" she asked.

"I do." She'd been a beautiful, compelling woman, at least five years older than he was, and they had both been seekers. They had both been ambivalent about church and church people, though they believed in God.

They had a brief, intense fling that they knew couldn't last. They were headed in opposite directions.

They spent a few minutes catching up, but soon, Will had had enough of small talk. He leaned closer to her. "I want you to explain what you did and why. How could you leave Eli on a doorstep?"

She sucked in a breath, and he realized that this encounter was taking a lot out of her. She had grown visibly more pale since they'd started talking, and her eyes were dim and weary. "I have pancreatic cancer," she said. "Just a few months to live."

"Oh, Athena." He looked into her eyes for a minute and then reached out to take her thin, birdlike hand, careful not to squeeze it. "I'm sorry. You're sure it's incurable?"

"Yes. I had a few treatments, but I wasn't a candidate for surgery. It's too advanced."

To think of Athena cut down in her prime just hurt. "Why didn't you tell me, though? Why didn't you tell me about Eli in the beginning? And why did you drop him off?"

"I didn't want social services involved." She shook her head. "No time for all that paperwork, and plus, I'm hooked on pain meds. I don't want anything to cut off my supply."

He shook his head. "I'm sure that hospice could give you all the pain meds that you need."

"Not really. I want the strong stuff."

A reluctant smile tugged at his mouth. "You always were countercultural."

"I'm still a rebel. Did a pretty good impression of a senior citizen, didn't I?"

He thought of her bundled up and arriving with the senior crowd, and smiled. But he had serious questions. "Why didn't you let me know I had a son, right from the beginning?"

She tilted her head as if trying to remember exactly what she'd been thinking. "I just didn't feel like it was your responsibility," she said finally. "I told you I couldn't get pregnant. That was what I thought. Eli was a sort of miracle baby."

Will fought to keep his voice steady, to be kind. "I still would have liked to know about him, get involved in his life. Didn't I have that right, as his father? Not to mention the financial support I could have provided you."

"I'm sorry." She met his eyes, and there was real regret in hers. "It was my mistake. I wanted to keep him to myself, and obviously, I shouldn't have."

She was tiring fast; he could see it in the way her chest moved rapidly up and down, in the high, feverish spots of color that appeared on her cheekbones.

"What do you want now?" he asked, keeping his voice gentle even though his emotions were roiling.

"Now that he's seen me, I guess… I guess I want to keep seeing him some."

"Of course. That would be good for both of you."

"But I just mean to visit. Will, he's yours, and you're going to be a great dad."

Will let out a harsh laugh. "Not hardly. Did you see that I knocked him down?"

"I did." She lifted her hands, palms up. "Most of us end up hurting other people now and then. It's part of the job description of being human. We can't let that disconnect us from others or we're doomed."

Her words were simple and direct, and they struck him to the core.

He watched a small gray bird land on the bush beside them, then flutter away. Behind him, the congregation was singing a praise song, its notes drifting out through the open windows.

His goal was to do no harm and to live in peace. He'd thought that meant isolating himself at his grandparents' farm. But now, Athena was suggesting that his goal was wrong.

"Everyone fails at parenting," she said. "Everyone. I mean, look at me. I left my child on your doorstep."

He nodded, listening.

"But we can also love, and with God's help, we can fix our mistakes."

From the church, another hymn rose up. This one was older: "Bringing in the Sheaves."

Athena cocked her head, listening. "I'm going to Jesus soon," she said, "but I can go in peace, knowing that you have Eli."

"Do you think they'll let me keep him?"

"Absolutely. Even if I weren't here to vouch for you, that whole group over at Abbott Farm would do it. You're well respected, Will, and well loved."

He looked at her wonderingly. "You think so?"

"Yes." She smiled at him, and then her shoulders slumped. "I need to go rest. Thanks for the talk."

"Of course." He hugged her carefully, gently, feeling the angles of her bones. He felt some peace, too. Maybe partly from being near the church, hearing the hymns. But also from being in the company of a fallible, wise, quirky woman.

"We'll talk soon," he promised. "Do you need a ride somewhere?"

She shook her head. "I'm paying a local girl to drive me. Promise me you'll get yourself together and go get your son."

He hesitated. Somehow, making a commitment to a dying woman meant he couldn't back out, no way.

"Promise me."

He nodded. "I promise."

"Good." She gave a little wave and wheeled off toward a van in the parking lot.

A young woman got out and helped her into the vehicle, then put the folded wheelchair in the back seat.

He watched them drive away, listened to the rising sound of music from the church.

Go get your son. The idea of it washed over him like clean water from a mountain spring.

He'd been given another chance. What had been utterly lost to him was now within his reach.

He drove the farm roads home, feeling gutted by what he'd learned. Vibrant, colorful Athena was not long for this world. It was inexpressibly sad.

And it left him confused, as confused as he'd felt when little Imad had tossed a bomb in his direction. What he'd thought about the child had changed, gotten vastly more complicated.

He'd just been purely mad at Eli's mother for dumping him on Will. But her decision had been complex. He still thought she was mistaken, but he could see why she'd done what she'd done.

She should have let him know about Eli, and she should have consulted with him about what to do when she'd gotten her diagnosis.

But he wouldn't berate her for it. He'd take the high ground because of her condition. Anyone with a heart would do that.

It brought home that life was short. Too short.

Athena had kept herself away from Eli for reasons he didn't fully understand, some of them seemingly selfish. He wasn't going to do that. He was going to go get Eli and find a way to parent him safely and well.

Was Will keeping himself away from Allie for wrong reasons, too? Would Eli have a lonely, motherless childhood for that reason?

Would Will, like Athena, die alone?

No. No, he wouldn't allow that to happen. He was going to get more counseling for his PTSD issues, until he was sure he could be safe around Eli and Allie. And then he'd apologize to Allie, apologize right, mend bridges.

And after that? He'd see what could be done.

21

Allie got through the next two weeks somehow. She kept busy with her work and spent time with the Flock.

Eli was back living with Will, and she saw them outside periodically, tossing a foam football or playing with Gus.

Will had written Allie a note and sent a couple of texts. He'd apologized for not answering the door and thanked her for all her help with Eli.

It sounded like goodbye.

Allie clung to her faith and the Flock. She didn't want it to hurt so badly every time she saw Will, but it did.

She hadn't answered his letter or texts. She didn't trust herself. But she returned his wave when she'd seen him in the yard. One day, when Gus had rolled around in something disgusting outside her tiny house, she'd bathed him and put him in Will's house.

She'd hugged Eli once, when he ran over to her, but then got in her car and drove away before Will could join them.

She just didn't want to reopen the door with him when he'd made it so clear he wasn't up for a relationship.

And she was.

She'd realized she wanted love and a family, and she'd been praying about it and talking to the pastor and to Jenn about it.

All along she'd been thinking that she wasn't lovable enough to have a family like other people. But she was learning, from what the pastor said, from the Bible passages he had her read, from Jenn's reassurances, that she *was* lovable. That God could love her, and maybe, just maybe, a husband could one day, too.

Tonight, Jenn was hosting a bonfire and pumpkin-carving party. She had hinted that she'd invite one or more eligible guys for Allie to meet. And no, Allie wasn't ready to date. Her feelings about Will were too strong and too raw. But she had to let that go, had to get herself out there and pursue her dreams. So she dressed in a cute flannel shirt and jeans and went.

When she reached Jenn's backyard, the fire was already roaring high. David and Eddie, Jenn's husband, were feeding the fire with the obvious intention of making it huge. Jenn was kneeling with her daughter, and Stone and Elena's girl of the same age, watching a pair of squirrels chase each other up and down the trunk of an oak tree.

They wouldn't have to worry about Ronald this time. After the police had investigated the trouble he'd caused at the Abbott Farm Open House, he'd been arrested for disturbing the peace. He'd been given a fine and sentenced to ninety days in jail.

In custody, he'd confessed that he'd overheard Will talking about his PTSD and, wanting to get back at him for chasing him off the farm, not once but twice, he'd fired the shot and it had had the effect he'd hoped for: it had messed with Will's head.

Ronald had meant to cause trouble, but God had worked it for good. Ronald's mischief had set off the chain of events that had led to Will almost losing Eli, and then to Athena revealing herself as Eli's mom.

Will seemed to be back all in with fathering Eli. In one of his texts, he'd let her know he was going to counseling. That was a good outcome.

Athena was staying at Pop's farmhouse, with a home-health nurse making frequent visits—the same nurse who'd helped with Ma Abbott. A pretty, silver-haired woman with a calming manner and an easy laugh.

Here they came now, bumping down to the bonfire, Athena in the chair, her nurse on one side and Pop on the other. They were immediately surrounded by the Flock, who had embraced Athena and made her feel a part of things. That was how they were. They were used to being outsiders themselves, and they didn't want other people to feel like outsiders, so they welcomed Athena like they would welcome any stranger in need.

When Will came over to the bonfire with Eli, Allie's heart nearly stopped.

She'd known, of course, that he'd be invited. But he looked so, so good in his faded jeans and the Henley shirt that clung to his chest and his muscular arms. His eyes met hers instantly, and she looked away. Then, ashamed, she looked back and smiled.

She had forgiven him. She'd forgiven him for pushing her away, not once but three times. He was a veteran. He had sacrificed for his country, and there were scars. He'd had a terrible experience with that mother and child and he still blamed himself. He'd been in firefights so awful that they'd given him PTSD. None of that was his fault.

So she didn't blame him, but she wasn't going to pursue him. He'd made it clear that he was too damaged for a relationship. He'd shown her who he was, and she had no choice but to believe him.

Still, she couldn't help stealing glances at him as he lifted Eli high in the air and then plunked him down at the table where several of the kids were painting pumpkins.

The adults hung around, chatting and helping the kids, drinking warm apple cider. The smell of wood smoke filled the air. Allie talked with everyone, determined not to be a downer, determined to look to the future and be positive.

After a while, Elena took all the kids to her house, and the nurse took Athena away.

"Pumpkin time for adults," Jenn said, clapping her hands to get everyone's attention. She'd set up sawhorse tables that didn't need to be kept clean, so they had fun cutting into the pumpkins, scooping out the slimy seeds, joking with memories of other pumpkins they'd carved in the past. It was the Flock all together, and now it was expanded to include partners.

Not for Allie. Not yet. Someday, though, she was determined she would have a life partner to bring to the Flock.

A whistle got everyone's attention. "We're going to do a pumpkin painting contest and surprise each other with what we carve or paint," Jenn announced. "Pop will be the judge. No peeking at anyone else's work."

Trust Jenn to make things fun.

They all got to work, shielding their creations from one another, joking and laughing. The fire crackled, and someone had turned on quiet guitar music. Jenn brought out extra sweatshirt and blankets for those who got chilled.

When time was up, they revealed what they'd done, one at a time. Jenn had painted flowers, of course. David, a covered bridge. Stone, a crude set of veggies. The spouses shared, too, and Pop Abbott made a show of examining each one, nodding and shaking his head.

Being the youngest, Allie revealed her pumpkin last. She was embarrassed because she'd painted kids, a bunch of them. The real meaning of the painting was that she wanted a bunch of kids of her own, but she could let it be thought that this was just about her being a kindergarten teacher.

"I'm all about the kids," she said.

Stone looked at her with narrowed eyes. "Get a husband first," he warned.

She rolled her eyes. "Of course."

"We didn't see what you carved, Will," Jenn said.

"I want Allie to see my pumpkins first," Will said. "I made two."

She looked at the first one. Painted in elegant script were the words *I'm sorry— forgive me?*

She shrugged, then managed a little smile and a nod toward Will.

He looked around the group. "I was neglectful toward Allie and pushed her away," he said. "It's not because I don't care for her. It's because I have some issues. But I'm working on them."

They all nodded. They, more than most people, knew about having issues.

"What's the other pumpkin?" Courtney asked.

Will looked around the group. "I might get some flak for this," he said. Then he spun the pumpkin around.

On it was a question: *Will you go out with me?*

Stone stood up quickly. "Hey, hey, I warned you about this."

"Yes, you did. But you don't get to make Allie's decisions. And, like I've told you multiple times, I've changed quite a bit since our early running-around days."

Stone frowned, then nodded. "You're right. You've changed, I can see it. And Allie has, too. She's a grown up."

That left Allie to answer the question,

but she was reeling. He'd invited her out on a date—in front of her family?

"I guess we can talk about it," she hedged. She wanted to go, for sure. But she also wanted to take care of herself.

"Tonight? Take a walk with me?"

Allie bit her lip. He was pushing, and it felt too soon.

But she'd wanted to put herself out there. She wanted a life partner, and Will was the man she cared for most, despite his quirks and flaws. "Okay," she said.

Half an hour later, they were walking down a country lane together. He took her hand and she let him. After a few minutes, he spoke. "I wanted to ask you more, but I didn't."

"What do you mean?" She looked up at him.

"I mean, I've fallen in love with you."

She sucked in air quickly. Did he mean it?

"Allie, I love you for your kind and upbeat nature and for your love of kids," he said. "And you're just so pretty. I look at you and I melt."

The words were romantic, but could she

believe them? She looked over at his handsome face and saw nothing but sincerity.

"The truth is, I don't just want to go out with you. I want to marry you."

She stared at him, barely able to breathe.

"It's true. I didn't want to ask you that, in front of your family. I knew I had to apologize first and get you to go out with me, but... will you consider it?"

Her heart was beating so hard she felt faint. "I thought we were ending things. I thought you couldn't be in a relationship."

"That was what I thought, too," he said, "but I've been talking to my counselor and praying about it. I've realized that punishing myself isn't the way to make a good contribution to the world. Plus, I can't just hide, alone, and expect that to heal me. I need to be with the woman I love—if she'll have me."

"I don't know." She sucked in air.

"You don't have to answer now," he said. "You shouldn't, not yet. I'm such a work in progress. Just tell me if I have a chance."

"I—yes. I'll consider it." Her heart was doing cartwheels in her chest.

He took both of her hands and looked

seriously down into her face. "Will you wear my ring while you do?"

"What?" She stared at him, stunned. Around them, the rise and fall of crickets chirping, the sound of the wind in the dry cornstalks, faded to nothing. He reached in his pocket, pulled out a box, and got down on one knee in the middle of the road. There, in the moonlight, he opened the box and held it up to her. "Allie, you don't have to answer this now, but I want the question to be out there. Will you marry me?"

She stood staring down at him, and she knew. She had to go for it. It was her chance for the brass ring. Her chance to have it all.

"I shouldn't answer yet, and I won't," she said. "But I'm pretty sure it's going to be a yes."

EPILOGUE

O*ne year later*

Allie was extra excited getting ready for today's class visit to Abbott Farm.

Eli's first grade class was coming—her own son's class—and Will, her husband, was a parent helper. They'd married in the summer, and the past months of being a family had been the best of her life.

Her foster siblings knew that today was special to her, so they were all participating in the visit. The farm stand would be a part of it, with David holding court. Jenn's flower fields and Stone's organics would all be part of the kids' activities.

They were the most supportive family ever, and living here in their midst was one of the best decisions Allie had ever made. Her confidence and belief in herself grew stronger every day because of their support.

And Will! She knew all of the Flock thought that their partners were amazing—and they were. But Will was that love she hadn't known she needed. So attractive that every time she saw him, her heart pounded faster. So comfortable that she always wanted to be around him. His quiet support, his unfailing care, offered her a warm nest of love unlike anything she'd ever known before. She was truly content. And there was more joy to come.

She took a deep breath and then plunged into the hectic preparations for a school visit. She greeted the three senior volunteers who would help with the kids and get some grandparent vibes going, greeted her siblings, made sure everything was in place. The yellow school bus rolled in, and kids began pouring out.

"Mommy!" Eli ran to her and threw himself into her arms. He was still young enough to love that his mom was here and in charge of the field trip. And yes, he called her Mommy now. Athena had died just two months after revealing the truth about her connection with Eli. Eli had spent time with Athena in those last months, and they'd taken lots of pictures to try to keep her memory alive for him. But he was a little boy, and he needed a mother now. A mommy who could bandage hurts, give him hugs, and cook his favorite foods.

Allie was honored to be that mommy.

The kids yelled and ran and basically went haywire until the teachers, plus Will and another parent helper, corralled them into order. Soon, different groups were busy at different stations. Some cut flowers for their families with Jenn. Others picked zucchini and yellow squash to take home, listening to Stone's rudimentary explanation of the growing process. Still another group went down to the farm stand and there learned about running a store.

Pop Abbott was there, mingling among the groups, talking about farming.

It was a great day, but Allie was tired by the end of it and not sorry to see them climb on the bus to head back to the school. Will and Eli didn't get on the bus; they were staying here at the farm, and they'd all go home together.

Allie sat down, tired but happy. She felt the warm autumn sun on her face and watched as Will threw a ball with Eli.

After a few minutes, Will came over to her. "You okay?"

"Yeah, I'm good," she said.

"You don't usually stay sitting this long," he said, sinking down beside her. "You must be tired after hosting all the kids."

There was so much love and trust between them now. She had the family she'd always wanted, and he had the peace he needed to do his work. But he was also fully involved with Eli, with her, and with the Flock, who were now his extended family.

"Actually, I'm more tired than usual," she said.

"Are you coming down with something?" He was solicitous as always, a true caretaker.

She leaned into him, and he put an arm

around her. "I have some news," she told him.

He shifted away to look at her face. "What's going on?"

"I, um, I did a pregnancy test today. I'm expecting."

She watched his face carefully to see his reaction. They had decided that they wanted as many kids as they could have, but she also knew that Will valued his time and freedom.

She needn't have worried. The joy on his face was real, completely unscripted. He picked her up and spun her around, then carefully placed her down on the hay bale. But their whoops brought the rest of the Flock to them. David and Courtney came over, between them the toddler they had adopted. They were excited because her biological mom was pregnant again and had agreed that they could adopt the next baby as well.

Jenn had just announced her own pregnancy.

Stone and Elena were here—and they'd recently announced that Elena was pregnant, too.

"What's going on?" Jenn asked.

"Good news," Allie said, unable to keep the grin off her face. "We're all gonna have babies together."

Immediately the air was filled with the shrieks of the women and the thumping sound of the men pounding Will's back.

"You too? That's amazing—something in the air or the water."

"It's Abbott Farm. It's a good place for a family. We all wanted families and found each other, and now we're growing."

Allie accepted hugs from her siblings and then stood with Will's arm around her, talking and enjoying the warm autumn breeze. There was peace in her heart and love for Will, and Eli, and all her family.

They'd come home to Orchard Springs and were going to build a life here. She lifted her face and sent up a heartfelt prayer of thanks.

HOME TO ORCHARD SPRINGS

GRAB THE WHOLE SERIES!

Wintertime Secrets: Jenn & Eddie.
The last man she wants to get snowed in with is her high school crush, now a single dad who's keeping a major secret...

Second Chance Springtime: David & Courtney.
Billionaire David Gonzalez never forgot his humble beginnings... nor the girl who broke his heart ten years ago.

A Secret Summer Child: Stone & Elena.
A struggling single mom must share a home with her all-too-appealing ex... without revealing he's the father of her child.

His Autumn Neighbor: Allie & Will
A handsome veteran, his best friend's little sister, and the child who shows up on the doorstep of the home they reluctantly share.

~

Turn the page to enjoy your bonus novella! *A Christmas Bond* kicks off Lee's bestselling Sacred Bond series.

BONUS NOVELLA: A CHRISTMAS BOND

SACRED BOND SERIES PREQUEL NOVELLA

1

December 23, 2000

ANNIE BAUER CLIMBED into her grandmother's ancient Buick Riviera inside the woman's dark, over-packed garage. She rested her head on the steering wheel and allowed herself thirty seconds of self-pity.

While her friends were back in Florida singing Christmas carols with their handsome husbands and adorable kids, she was in a dangerous, run-down neighborhood in freezing-cold Pittsburgh. No husband and kids of her own and none in sight, now that she was thirty-five. She and Gran would be spending Christmas alone. Gran was a huge blessing, but the woman who'd raised her was starting to need more help than Annie could give from across the country, and that worried her.

Enough with the complaining. She wrestled the car's balky gearshift into reverse, let out the clutch, and eased the giant vehicle carefully out of the garage. Amazing that the thing would even run, as rarely as Gran drove it. Now, if Annie could just get it to the end of the driveway without stalling, they'd have room to locate the yard nativity scene and drag it out.

Thump. *Crash*. Annie's heartbeat jumped as a gang of teenage boys, all shouting and catcalling, banged on the car's windows. Their hats and ski masks covered most of their faces, making them look inhuman.

Fear flooded her and she accidentally gunned the gas pedal. She jolted backward down the ice-rutted driveway.

The sound of crunching metal and splintering wood filled the air. The car bumped over something and she screamed.

She jolted to a stunned halt in the middle of the street, heart still racing. Who or what had she hit?

Frantic, she lifted up in the seat to look at the driveway she'd just emerged from.

Whew. No bodies.

The teenagers were running toward her, and she knew they were dangerous, that she needed to lock the old car's doors, but she was frozen in place.

"Hey! Hey! You okay?"

A man's voice penetrated her panic and she turned to the window, fogging it with her breath. She made out the face of her grandmother's neighbor, dark eyebrows raised over warm brown eyes.

John Moretti. Great.

But even though he was one of the most annoying men she knew, it was a relief to see him. She turned off the car, opened the door, and climbed out into the cold.

Immediately, she was surrounded by an indistinguishable mass of loud-talking, rough-looking teens, and she felt the panic rising again and looked for John.

"Boys! Everything's fine. Go let Miss Clara know that Annie's okay and help her back into the house. Make sure she doesn't fall."

"Is Gran all right?" Concerned, she looked toward the house to see her grandmother halfway down the front steps, holding the railing with one hand and her cane with another. At the window, Gran's little brown-and-white terrier barked hysterically.

Annie took a step toward her grandmother, but John put a hand on her arm. "She's fine. The boys will help get her inside."

"Are the boys gang members, or just your delinquents?"

John narrowed his eyes. "They attend the Covenant School. They're decent kids who like your grandma and are happy to help her." He paused, then added with a wry smile, "Especially if she gives them cookies."

"Which she will." Annie drew in a breath and let it out in a sigh as her fears calmed. *Okay. Pull yourself together. Damage control.* "What did I hit?" She headed toward the back of the car on still-shaky legs.

John walked beside her, not touching her, just being a presence—a strong, tall presence—and she had to admit it made her feel better. "You hit a mailbox, but I doubt if this tank even got a scratch. Why were you driving it?"

She bent down to examine the rear bumper. It looked fine, maybe one extra dent added to many others, so she straightened. "Gran insists that we get out the nativity scene and put it up in the yard. It's all stored back behind the car, so I was just pulling it out...well. Better get it back in the driveway." She approached the driver's door with a grimace of distaste. "This thing has a mind of its own."

"Want me to try driving it?" John sounded as eager as a teenager. "I haven't had my hands on one of these babies since I was a kid."

The sprinkling of grey in his hair was her only indication that he was probably over forty. She didn't like what the man was doing to the neighborhood, but she did trust him to drive the car. "Surc, but you might want to check on your decent kids first. Two of them went off-task." She gestured toward the shortest, stockiest of the boys, who stood near the pines at the edge of Gran's yard, lighting a cigarette. Another boy, young-looking beneath the swagger, hesitated halfway between the smoker and the two who were helping Gran up the porch steps.

Before John could speak, Gran turned, spotted the two missing teenagers, and called in her reedy voice. "Boys! I have coffeecake just out of the oven. Come have a slice."

Annie shuddered at the thought of those delinquents swarming inside Gran's house. Her little dog wouldn't exactly provide protection. For the millionth time, she wondered how Gran did it, how she'd managed to forgive the past and open herself to hurt and risk again.

The Lord had to love her grandma for connecting with these boys. That was what they needed, a friend.

Unfortunately, Annie herself wasn't that good of a person. Ever since the horror of Rhonda's death, she'd despised gangs of teenagers. She wasn't going to be that friend.

"Come on, Rock, you can smoke later." The tallest boy was looking over his shoulder, his arm crooked for Gran to hold onto.

The smoker dropped his cigarette into

the snow and sauntered toward the house, followed by the other one who'd stayed in the yard. Nice.

"Problem solved," John said cheerfully.

Annie lifted an eyebrow at him. "For now."

~

Forget about her, John told himself as he eased the vehicle back into the driveway, parking it in front of the garage. *It's Christmas and you're lonely, but that doesn't mean you need to chase after a younger woman like Annie.*

He sat a minute in the old car as memories assailed him. It had been just such a car that he'd driven to take out Emily on their first date. Back in, when was it, eighty-five? Even then the vehicle had been ten years old, but he'd been as proud as punch to have a nice big car in which to take out a college girl and show her the townie side of life.

It had been in just such a car that he'd made the biggest mistake of his life, one he was still paying for. And still nursing that same old flame.

He got out of the car and handed the

keys to the pretty lady in front of him, feeling that stirring again. Nope. Not doing that, he told his hormones. He was forty and counting, but he was still a man with a man's desires, even though he rarely allowed himself to act on them.

"I'll go get my tools and give you a hand with that mailbox," he offered, and left before she could answer. Before he could get tangled up again in how attractive she was. Blonde hair down past her shoulders and a knockout figure that showed up real pretty in her snug jeans and green sweater.

Yeah, he'd been checking her out ever since he'd started renovating the run-down former apartment building that had become the Covenant School. He'd argued with her in neighborhood meetings about whether the boys at the school would be a threat to the block's elderly residents. He'd noticed her visiting her Grandma more frequently lately, trimming bushes and hiring a neighborhood kid to cut the grass in the summer, raking leaves in the fall.

Despite a little bit of online stalking, though, he didn't know much about her, except that she had a job in PR somewhere in south Florida and had never been married. Which was a red flag, even though it was one he bore himself. Every woman he'd dated wanted to know why he'd never settled down. Now that PTSD was a known thing, sensitive ladies blamed his stints in Beirut and Grenada, and he let them think so. It was a better story than the truth.

He entered his room, on one end of the Covenant School and his cat, Whiskers, sauntered over to greet him. He knelt to run his hands along her back and was rewarded with a sharp nip.

"Biting the hand that feeds you, Whiskers?" He stood and headed to get his tools. Lately he'd been having way too many conversations with his cat. A chance to hang out with a real live beautiful blonde, even if she was off limits, was a better way to spend Christmas week.

ANNIE TALKED to the mail carrier and reassured a couple of the neighbors that she and Gran's car were okay. Then she headed up to the house just as the gang of four came out.

"You boys have a wonderful Christmas," Gran was saying to them, insisting on hugging each one.

As they took off after John, Gran turned to Annie with a brilliant smile. "You'll help me pull out the crèche, now, won't you?"

"Oh, Gran, do you really want to do the whole yard thing? It's so close to Christmas, and we'll just have to put it back..."

"I would have done it earlier if you'd been here to help me," Gran reminded her. "Besides, when is the right time for the Christ child but at Christmas?"

"Of course, of course." Annie waved a hand, not wanting Gran to go on one of her Christian rants. Annie went to church sometimes, but lately, it had all grown stale.

Everything had grown stale.

She shook off her despondency and forced cheer into her voice. "Okay, come on, let's get to it. Where's the stuff?"

Fifteen minutes later they'd uncovered the old wooden cradle in Gran's impossible heap of yard-ware, and Annie vowed once again to organize her Gran's garage. Gran loved to decorate and continued to do so in every season, her house often the only spot of light on a dark street in an increasingly bad neighborhood.

Well, some would say the school next door was another source of light, but Annie disagreed. It was a threat, bringing delinquent boys from all over the country into the city.

At least now they were mostly gone home for Christmas. "How come there are some boys left at that awful school?" She set the crèche carefully into place.

"Covenant School isn't awful. For one thing, they've renovated a run-down old apartment building and brought it to life again. This neighborhood needs all the help it can get."

"And the boys?" Annie had begun to notice Gran's tendency to go off track. "Why are they here?"

"I don't suppose they have homes to go to. Oh, look, there's that John coming this way. I like that man. You should go out with him."

"Gran!" Annie felt her cheeks heating. Back in Florida, her extremely limited dating life involved professional, classically handsome men in suits. John, with his three-day stubble and bodybuilder muscles and workmanlike clothes, was definitely not her type. "Is he single?"

"Yes, he is." Gran's eyes sparkled, and Annie hoped she'd get John's story, but instead, Gran's eyes lit on the wrapped bundle in the crèche. "Let's look at Baby Jesus," she said, taking up the doll and crooning over it. "Isn't he beautiful? Do you know, this was your mother's doll."

"It was Mom's?" Annie took the doll and looked at it. Plastic molded hair, indeterminate gender, swaddled in blankets.

"Yes, and that's why I treasure it."

Annie cuddled the doll close, thinking of her beautiful, vulnerable mother. Her throat went tight.

"Here to fix your mailbox, ladies." John approached with a metal toolbox in one hand. Despite the cold, he was bare-headed, dressed in a leather jacket and jeans.

"What on earth is wrong with my mailbox?'

Annie felt a twist of worry as she looked at her grandmother. Ten minutes ago she'd seen Annie hit the mailbox and five minutes ago they'd discussed it.

Was Gran okay here, living alone? With a bunch of delinquents next door? Although having John here was a blessing, obviously.

"Nothing's wrong that can't be fixed. You just let me handle it, Miss Clara, all right?" He patted the older woman's arm.

"You go help him, Annie. I think it's time for my afternoon lie-down."

"Want me to come fix you some tea, Gran?"

"Oh, no, indeed." Gran turned and headed up the stairs, waving off Annie's offer of assistance.

Annie followed John down to the wreck of a mailbox, frowning at the splintered wood and bent metal. "Have you noticed my grandma going downhill recently?"

"Hold this," he said. "Right there, real steady." He'd pushed the mailbox upright and was examining the point where the two pieces of the post came together.

She did as he said, watching as his strong hands seemed to read the wood. Sometimes it seemed like everything she did, working in PR and advertising, amounted to exactly nothing. Doing things with your hands, fixing an old woman's mailbox, now that was something tangible. She liked that.

"She's seeming a little confused at times," he said around a mouthful of nails. "That's why the boys came rushing over when they saw the car backing out."

"It's enough for them to notice?"

He nodded. "Believe it or not, they're pretty sensitive. Both Rock and Daniel have older relatives who played a big role in their raising."

"I'm sorry I judged them, but they should be a little more aware. I don't like having the school here, John. Those four may be okay—though I have my doubts about the one who smokes—but I'm sure you have more criminal elements during the year."

"Nope, these are my worst," he said cheerfully. He pulled a metal brace out of his tool box and wrapped it around the broken post. "This is a temporary measure. Come spring, we'll want to dig out the old post and put in a whole new replacement."

"How do you keep boys like that in control? Is my Gran at risk of being robbed?"

"Doubt they'd steal from her, because

she's taken the step of connecting with them. It's what they need most of all." He paused, then met her eyes with his own intense chocolate ones, framed by lines that said he'd been around awhile, had seen a lot and done a lot. "What we all need, right?"

Their gazes held for a beat too long, and suddenly Annie wasn't sure what they were talking about. She looked down at the mailbox post. "Thanks for doing this. I really appreciate it. I appreciate your keeping an eye on Gran, too." She forced herself to take a breath and stop talking.

"It's no problem. She's a good neighbor."

For no reason she could understand, Annie felt winded. "So are you. You got it now? I'd better go in."

2

ANNIE SNUGGLED DEEPER into the thick quilts. Only her nose stuck out, and it was cold, but the rest of her was deliciously warm. She'd slept well. Something about this cool, not-very-well insulated house, the sound of cars crunching over snow, the slant-roofed ceiling of her old room—it all took her back to happy childhood days.

A small, warm body wiggled against her, and she reached down to draw Gran's dog up to her chest, cuddling him like a baby. "Macy! You slept with me?"

Macy licked Annie's face and rolled over on his back for a belly rub.

Annie obliged, drawing in a deep breath. *Mmm.* What was that smell? Could Gran be cooking bacon?

A smile curved her mouth as she squinted at the winter sun shining around the cracks of the window blinds. She didn't have to get up and go to a job that was super stressful, fighting the sharks, standing up for womankind, proving her toughness. For once, she could relax and be a kid again.

And Christmas was coming!

A rhythmic bang-bang-bang intruded on her hazy, half-asleep thoughts.

Bang. Scrape. Bang.

What the heck was that? She tried to snuggle back in, but now that she'd taken notice of the noise outside, it bothered her. She flung off the bedding and padded to the window in the thick socks she'd slept in, dragging a quilt with her. She raised the blind and frowned.

Outside were teenage boys.

An alarming number of boys, in heavy jackets, shoveling Gran's sidewalk and driveway and yelling insults at each other. Were they the same ones from yesterday?

It was good of them to help Gran, but the

sight of an unsupervised gang of teenagers made her stomach churn with painful memories. So much for a peaceful morning. She threw the blanket back down onto the bed, stepped into yesterday's jeans and a sweater she found in her old closet, and dragged a brush through her hair.

When she opened her bedroom door, the good smell increased. Bacon, and was that... cinnamon rolls? Maybe hot chocolate?

She hurried down the stairs, Macy trotting along behind her, and found her grandmother, in a robe and old-lady curlers, frying bacon at the stove.

"Good morning, honey. I fixed your favorite breakfast."

Annie wrapped her arms around the woman who'd pretty much raised her and her sister while her mom had worked, who'd sacrificed her peaceful retirement to deal with temperamental teens. "You're amazing, Gran."

"Now, you just sit down while I pour you some juice."

"I'll get it, thanks." She opened the fridge and rummaged among the cartons until she found an orange juice that wasn't expired.

"What do you think of the boys shoveling your driveway for you?"

"They're wonderful young men."

"It's nice they do that," Annie admitted, "but they're delinquents, right? That's why they're at that school."

"Oh, well, a little delinquency never hurt anyone," her gran said, apropos of nothing. "Honey, could you let Macy out?"

Annie turned toward the door only to see the small brown and white dog squat down with obvious purpose. "Macy!" she yelled and ran to grab the dog before he made a puddle. She opened the door hastily, still in her socks, and nudged the reluctant creature outside.

The sight of the snow-cloaked neighborhood made her smile. Christmas in Florida couldn't compare. She took in a deep breath of crisp, cold air.

There was a warning shout, and then a couple of boys on a makeshift cardboard-box sled crashed into Macy, making him yelp and jump back.

"Hey!" Annie rushed out with no coat, wet cold seeping into her sock-clad feet, and swept the small animal into her arms. Carefully, she checked him for damage. "Watch where you're going!" she yelled at the laughing boys who'd tumbled off the sled into the snow.

Macy wiggled out of her arms, obviously fine, and forgetting the reason he was outside in the first place, she let him back in the house, casting one last head-shake back at the irresponsible boys. You had to shut down kids like that. They were a lot more dangerous than they looked.

Macy trotted back into the house, looked up at Annie, and squatted.

"Macy!" Annie rolled her eyes and grabbed a roll of paper towels.

"Goodness, what's the matter?" her grandma asked. "Macy never has accidents. Well, almost never. Here, dear." She handed Annie a mostly used bottle of Pet Spot Cleanup, belying her words.

Macy flopped contentedly down in his dog bed.

"It's fine, Gran." Annie finished the cleanup and then washed her hands at the old white enamel sink. "Look, I'm going to run outside and kinda supervise those boys. I don't like them hanging around here."

"Whatever you think, dear. There's a shovel in the garage." Gran paused and a twinkle came into her eyes. "Maybe you'll get a chance to shovel alongside John."

"Why would I want that?" Annie's face heated.

"He's a very nice man. But a little lonely." Gran put her hand on Annie's arm. "Which is the way I'd characterize you, too, dear. I'd like to see you meet someone and settle down."

"Enough with the matchmaking." She frowned at Gran with mock-sternness as she headed for the coat closet. John was the guy who'd argued for the Covenant School to come to this neighborhood. He was her enemy, not any kind of a romantic prospect.

Minutes later, Annie was outside working on the front walk. The boys, she noticed, stayed away from her; they'd moved on to another neighbor's driveway, leaving Gran's half undone.

Fine with her. She shoveled rhythmically, enjoying the exercise The air cooled her nostrils and her cheeks felt chilled, but the rest of her was warm from exertion. It was a good feeling, taking her back to her younger days.

They'd been happy, she and Rhonda, living here with Mom and Gran. She needed to remember the good times, stop focusing on the bad stuff.

"Annie, is that you in there?" The cheerful male voice came from right beside her, making her jump.

She peered out from the hood of Gran's jacket. "John! You scared me."

"I'm sorry. I just wanted to apologize for the boys running into the dog. They told me about it."

"They should watch where they're going. Macy could've been hurt."

"Exactly what I said." His voice was gentle, designed to soothe. "You look nice."

Annie looked down at her old jeans. She was wearing Gran's ancient jacket and boots. "Really? Checked your eyes lately?"

"My eyes are fine." Indeed, they sparkled nicely as he gazed at her. "I may be a little older than you are, but I can still see well enough to recognize a beautiful woman."

Whoa. He thought she was beautiful? She felt her cheeks warming up.

She didn't know what to say, though. She never flirted, rarely dated, never had full-on relationships. At thirty-five years old, she just wasn't comfortable with men. Hadn't been, really, since Rhonda had died.

John fell into companionable shoveling beside her, apparently unaware of her relationship shortcomings. Which left her time to notice the strength and steadiness with which he worked, and the way the snow twinkled in his dark hair.

They worked together for a while, getting the rest of the driveway shoveled. She was just feeling regretful about the fact that they'd soon part when a snowball hit her square in the head. She let out a startled cry, dropping her shovel. Another snowball hit her hard on the shoulder and she stepped back and staggered right into a snowdrift.

"Hey!" John yelled at whoever had thrown the snowball. "You boys get over here and apologize." He turned to her, reached out a strong hand, and pulled her upright. "I'm sorry. Are you okay? I suspect those snowballs were aimed at me."

But as the boys approached, they seemed to morph into the bullies who'd mercilessly tormented her sister on the way home from school each day. She backed away, raising her hands, her heart racing. "Get away! Go!"

She turned and rushed toward the house, knees shaking. Teenage boys in groups were capable of just about anything.

JOHN SAW HIS BOYS' reaction to Annie's obvious fear of them. Stereotypes hurt, and the evidence of that was there in Zeke's slow, disbelieving head shake, in Rock's curled lip.

Boone shrugged it off and turned away, obviously hardened to being treated like a bad kid, but Daniel looked crushed. Although Daniel had grown up in the system right here in Pittsburgh, he was sensitive. Smart as a whip and easily the best-looking of all the boys, he loved movies and reading, and he was already a hit with the high school girls. But he tended toward depression. As soon as Christmas was over, John was going to have the boy see a doctor, maybe get on some medication.

Meanwhile, he didn't need to be put down. None of them did.

John's stomach churned. Where did Annie get off treating his boys like lowlifes?

He stomped through the snow after her. "Hey! Hey!"

She didn't even acknowledge him. Instead, she hurried up the porch stairs and banged through the door into the house.

His blood pounding, John strode up after her. "Hey!"

She slammed the door in his face.

Whoa. Nobody disrespected John Moretti. He banged a fist on the door, hard and repeatedly.

Miss Clara's dog yipped madly. When he looked through the window on the side of the doorway, he didn't see the annoying Annie. Instead, he saw Miss Clara, her expression a mixture of concern and alarm that would have been comical if it didn't make him feel ashamed.

He turned away and saw four young faces looking up at him.

Drawing in a calming breath, John shot up a prayer for help. What exactly was he modeling to these boys?

Settling down and leaving wasn't enough. He had to apologize.

"Keep shoveling, boys. Show's over." But it wasn't, he thought as he tapped gently on the door and waved through the window, a conciliatory smile on his face. Only the good part was. Now, it was time for this low-life to grovel.

Miss Clara opened the door. "Come on in, John. Mercy, I thought you were going to knock the house down. What's going on?"

"Yeah." He rubbed the back of his neck, hot under his leather jacket. "Sorry about that." He bent down to pick up the little dog that was jumping at his leg. "I…wondered if I could speak with Annie."

"Of course! " A smile broke out over Miss Clara's face. "Although you may have to do a little fancy footwork. She didn't look happy. What happened out there?"

"My boys hit her with a snowball. Then had the nerve to laugh."

"Oh, dear." Miss Clara was helping him out of his jacket, which was ridiculous. "Let me hang this up. You just relax. I'll get her to come downstairs."

"It's ok if she doesn't…"

"No, no. She will. That girl needs to have some fun in her life. She's, well, she's touchy, you see. This time of year is hard for her."

He wanted more explanation, but the

older woman was already walking carefully up the wooden staircase.

Still holding the dog, he looked around at the house, the same era and style as the Covenant School, and yet so different. Miss Clara's woodwork was painted, and flowered curtains hung at every window. The kitchen table had to be ancient, with its red top and chrome edging and legs. His own grandma had had such a table.

He settled into one of the kitchen chairs and put the dog down, drawing in smells that reminded him of childhood Christmases, all cinnamon and ginger. Such a peaceful place, but not for long. Why had sophisticated, confident, professional Annie Bauer freaked out on him and his boys like that?

"Here she is!" Miss Clara's brilliant smile and triumphant voice made it seem like she'd produced a white rabbit out of a hat. "Now, I had these rolls staying warm in the oven. Why don't you just sit down and have some. Annie can pour coffee. I'm just going to go upstairs and...have a little rest."

"Thank you," he said as Miss Clara set a

dish of amazing-looking, fragrant cinnamon rolls on the table.

'You're welcome, dear. Enjoy." She hurried out of the room and made her way up the stairs again.

He turned to her granddaughter. "Annie, I'm sorry for what the boys did. Whether or not they intended to hit you with those snowballs, they knocked you over and I'm going to make them apologize."

"Please don't." She leaned back against the counter, twisting her hands together, not meeting his eyes. "I don't want to talk to them."

Her attitude rankled. "Why not? Because they're rough around the edges? Poor kids?"

"No, because they're junior criminals. Nothing good's going to come out of my speaking with them." She crossed her arms, half-turning away.

Her subtext wasn't particularly hidden—nothing good was going to come out of her connecting with him, either.

He looked around to make sure Miss Clara was out of earshot. "Look," he said, "we don't have to be friends, but I'd appreciate your cutting my boys a break. This is their last chance before juvie. I'm working my...my *tail* off trying to keep them on the straight and narrow. Your treating them like dangerous criminals doesn't help."

"I'm sorry," she said tonelessly.

"Is it all right if they come over here and apologize?"

"No!" She gripped the counter behind her. "I'd rather they just stay away. Here," she added, walking to the table and thrusting the plate of cinnamon rolls into his hands, "take these to the boys. I just can't deal."

He took the rolls and she instantly turned and left the room. "Well, okay then," John said, disgusted. "I'll let myself out."

~

LATER THAT NIGHT, he and the boys were relaxing in front of a football game in the school's common room, eating spaghetti and meatballs and garlic bread, when there was an angry banging on the building's front door.

"I'll get it," he said, not that the teenagers were showing any eagerness to jump up. He couldn't blame them; he'd worn them out good today shoveling, and then lectured them about their snowball throwing.

Plus, there was some gang activity in the neighborhood. He'd just as soon answer the door himself, keep the boys from being targets.

But it wasn't a gang member, he realized as he opened the door. It was Annie.

"Come on in," he said. Hopefully, she'd relented and was here to let the boys apologize and maybe connect with her a little. But from the angry look in her eyes, it didn't seem likely. Didn't this gal ever lighten up?

"I want to talk to your boys," she said, her voice quivering.

"About what?" He stood in the entryway, his own bulky body serving as a block between her and the boys in his care.

"They stole Baby Jesus," she said, "and I want him back."

3

ANNIE WAS FUMING. "I want to talk to them."

"What about Baby Jesus?" John cocked his head to one side, looking at her as if she'd lost her marbles.

"You should have seen Grandma Clara. We'd just gotten back from the store, and she wanted to see the crèche. So we go down to the street, tromping through the snow and ice, which isn't easy when you're close to ninety." She felt a flash of guilt, since John and his boys were the ones who cleared Gran's driveway most of the time, but she stifled it and focused on her anger. "And there's the manger, empty. Well, she looked at that and she started to cry." Her own voice broke at the memory.

He shook his head emphatically. "No way would my boys steal from Miss Clara."

Annie's blood pressure shot up. "Of course they would. They're troublemakers. That's why I didn't want them in the neighborhood."

"Listen." He crossed his arms over his broad chest. "I'm having a real hard time liking you right now."

She lifted her hands, palms up. "Do I look like I care? Listen, that beat up old doll she uses for a Baby Jesus means the world to my grandma, and I want it back. Let me talk to those boys." She didn't want to be a total witch about this, but it had taken all the courage she had to come over here after dark and confront a bunch of guys. It wasn't her thing. It wasn't easy for her. She was a wreck, in fact, but if she wanted to get the Jesus doll back, she'd have to go through with it.

Something of that must've shown in her face, because the big man in front of her seemed to relent. "Well, listen. I'll let you talk to them, but on one condition."

"What's that?'

"That you have a plate of Moretti spaghetti with us first. Watch a little bit of the game."

"Why?"

"Because it seems to me you need to get to know these boys a little bit before you judge them."

Those words hit her like a brick to the head. She *was* being awful, being the kind of person she didn't even like, being judgmental. And here this man was offering her food. It was Christmas, and she sure wasn't being a very good Christian.

She closed her eyes, took a deep breath.

And realized that whatever John was cooking smelled amazing. "You're right. I'm sorry. Okay."

She followed him into a large kitchen with a professional-level stainless steel stove. The fridge was industrial sized as well. "You do a lot of cooking in here?"

He chuckled. "I'm too busy most of the time, but when it's vacation and the staff is off, yeah, I cook." He winked at her. "That's just one of the benefits of us Italian men. We know how to cook."

She blushed, but he wasn't looking at

her; he was dipping her out a huge plate of spaghetti and scooping salad into a bowl. “Water or pop?” he offered. “I don’t keep alcohol in the house.”

“Because of the boys?”

“Partly.” He studied her face as if gauging her capacity to understand. “Teenage boys can easily get started on bad habits. I know that because I started drinking then, myself. It got to be a problem later, and now I don’t touch it. *Can’t* touch it.”

Oh. Interesting. “I’ll have water, and John…” She put a hand on his arm. “Thanks for being kind. I overreacted a bit and I’m sorry.”

He looked into her eyes and their gazes danced together for a second too long. She turned away.

“In here,” he said, and led the way into a ragged lounge where four boys slumped on worn leather couches watching a large screen TV.

“Men. We have a lady present.”

To her shock, they all stood up and greeted her, offering their hands. Who did that in the North, these days? Not that they made eye contact, but still. Impressive.

As she savored the thick marinara sauce on perfect *al dente* spaghetti noodles, her eyes kept shifting back to John. He talked about the game to the boys, not a lot, but enough that each one got a little bit of attention if he wanted it. He refilled her water glass once and got her some parmesan cheese. When one of the boys cursed at a bad play, he quelled it with a loudly cleared throat and a pointed look at the boy and then at her. She suspected he'd have let it go if there wasn't a guest present.

Her irritation about the school and the boys was dissolving into curiosity. What life circumstances had led to him spending Christmas taking care of boys who didn't have a home? Why didn't *he* have a wife, a girlfriend, children? Was he as lonely as she was?

It was hard to believe a man like John had no choice but to be alone. He wasn't conventionally handsome, exactly, but he had a charm and male energy that made him appealing. Then again, there was something guarded about him, a distance behind the cheerful, quick-with-a-joke façade that probably wouldn't be easy to breach.

The game ended at about the same time that she finished her spaghetti. "Thank you," she said to John. "That was fantastic."

"You're welcome." He clicked the TV off. The boys started to get up, but he raised a hand. "Sit down a minute. Ms. Bauer wants to talk to you about something."

Annie's heart pounded as she looked at the unsmiling boys, so similar to those who'd tormented her sister in their teenage years. Then she pictured her grandmother crying, and that gave her courage. "Someone stole the Baby Jesus from my grandma's manger."

One of them snickered, then quickly stifled the sound. The younger looking one. Not the smoker.

"Do you know something about it, Boone?" John asked.

The boy shook his head rapidly. "No, sir," he said, and Annie noticed a southern accent.

"We wouldn't steal from Miss Clara," Zeke, the oldest one, said. "She's treated us real well."

Rock looked away.

"Daniel? Rock?"

"Not me." Daniel, an exceptionally handsome teenager, lifted both his hands.

"I ain't got no use for Jesus." Rock stood up, shoved his hands in his pockets, and turned away. "Going outside."

"Okay if we go too, sir?" Boone grinned. "Unless you two need us to chaperone you."

John narrowed his eyes at the snickering group. "Stay on our block and be inside by 10:00. You know the rules."

She watched the boys leave. "I'm not sure I trust them. Especially Rock."

John heaved a sigh. "Me too. Especially Rock. He worries me." It was obvious that his worry went deeper than anything that had happened today. "Kid has a lot of heart underneath all that swagger. I've been lifting weights with him, using it as an excuse to get some quiet time away from the other boys. He can't escape hearing about Jesus when I'm holding two-hundred and twenty-five pounds of barbell over that hard head of his."

So that was where John got his extremely nice muscles. "I really admire that you—"

"Tell me about your—"

They'd spoken at the same time, and

they both stopped and laughed awkwardly. Suddenly, Annie felt a warm tension in the room.

"I'm gonna look into it, Annie. I'll find out something from the boys, if there's anything to find out. Sometimes it just takes a little time for them to..."

"To 'fess up?" She stood abruptly, not patient with excuses about the boys and inexplicably uncomfortable. "I should go home. Get back to Gran."

"Of course. I'll walk you there."

"There's no need to do that." She found her coat where he'd hung it on an old-fashioned coat tree, and before she could shoulder into it, John was there, holding it for her.

She felt his firm hand as he tucked it around her shoulders, and her breath caught. A confident man with good manners. She'd encountered that rarely, and she liked it. Found it sexy.

She spun toward the door, needing to get away from this man's effect on her, because he was obviously doing crazy things to her mind. Maybe it was the season, maybe it was loneliness, but she felt like she could fall for John. Fall right into an affair with him.

And that would be totally inappropriate. His being a little older didn't scare her; it probably contributed to his confidence and to his good manners, his knowledge of how to treat a woman that so few men her own age seemed to share. But it also brought up a few memories in her mind. She'd fallen for an older guy once before.

With disastrous consequences.

They headed down the stairs, and he offered her his arm. Since the sidewalk was slippery, she took it, clinging to the leather, feeling his steadiness. He was strong in more ways than one.

"Look up," he said, "it's gotten clear."

Sure enough, the sky was a collection of stars—glowing pinpoints, with a sliver of a moon off to the side of the navy blue sky. The air was crisp, freezing her nostrils, and she huddled a little closer to John without even thinking about it. Wow.

Too soon, they'd reached her gran's house.

"Can I see the nativity scene?" His breath made clouds.

"Sure." She led him over to the yard and they tromped through the snowdrifts. Gran had turned on the spotlight, and the manger scene showed in its glory, with an empty straw manger.

"What a shame," he said.

"She uses a doll that belonged to my mother."

"Your mother's passed?"

She nodded, suddenly unable to speak.

"I'm sorry," he said. "My folks are gone, too."

They were quiet a minute, and a rare sense of peace and connection stole over Annie. What was it about this man?

"It's nice that Miss Clara puts up decorations," he commented finally. "A lot of people have stopped doing it."

"Or don't bother," she said, nudging him and smiling.

"Hey, I put up a couple of wreaths! Give me a break, I'm dealing with maintaining that old building and babysitting four teenagers."

They were both laughing a little, and then their eyes met, and the laughter stopped.

Annie caught her breath at his expression. She turned her face away, feeling awkward.

"Hey." He touched her chin, causing her to look back at him. "You're a very pretty lady."

His voice sounded practiced, like he was moving into seasoned flirt mode, and she took a step back. "Don't do that, John."

"Do what?"

"Don't come on to me like you've come on to dozens of other women."

He raised an eyebrow. "What makes you think I've done that?"

"Are you kidding? A charmer like you?" she said. "Just a hunch."

"Um, thank you. I think." She noticed he didn't deny it.

And she had to defend herself, couldn't let herself give in to that friendly magnetism. "I don't enjoy feeling like one of a crowd."

He chuckled. "Tell my cat about the crowds of women beating down my door." He clasped her hands, and through her gloves, she could feel his strength and decisiveness. "I've been alone for a good long while. Just haven't felt like pursuing anyone. You might be changing my mind, though."

She opened her mouth to protest, but he touched her lips with a finger and she lost her breath.

"Anyway, the past is the past and this is now, and you're a special lady."

He was looking at her hard again, and she didn't know how to react, didn't know what to do. Was he going to kiss her?

He kept watching her eyes, and very deliberately, he removed her glove, lifted her hand to his lips, and kissed it, never letting go of her gaze.

Heat flooded Annie's body and she felt herself starting to go soft, heart melting, body yielding, resistance fading. On the verge of giving in entirely to his appeal, panic welled up.

Letting those melting, romantic feelings overcome her was way too dangerous. It had blinded her to danger once before, but she couldn't let that happen again.

She pulled her hand away. "Don't think you can charm me," she said, even though that was exactly what he'd been doing. "I'm not that easy to distract. I want to know what happened to my grandma's doll. I think one of your boys took it."

John recoiled, looking startled. "I'm not trying to distract you. I just felt..."

"To you it's just a beat-up baby doll, but it means something to my family."

John lifted his hands, palms up. "I never said it didn't."

"Forget it. Not every woman's going to fall under your leather-jacket spell, John."

His faced clouded. "You're attributing way too much motive to what seemed like a nice walk under the stars with a beautiful lady."

"Stop it!" Frustrated with herself for liking the way he called her beautiful, she lashed out. "If you don't figure out which of those boys took it, the police will."

Her attack had him looking shell-shocked. Well, good.

He opened his mouth, closed it, stared off toward the school, then spoke. "Annie," he said, "please don't call the police. Those boys are one step away from juvie. Any run-in with the law is likely to put them straight into the kind of place they'll never recover from."

She squared her jaw. This felt more comfortable, being harsh, stepping away. It felt safer. She crossed her arms over her chest. "Then you'd better find out what other mischief they're up to. I expect to hear some answers by tomorrow. We want that doll back by Christmas."

And once they had the doll back, she could forget about John Moretti. She needed to be far, far away from this man who evoked such dangerous feelings in her.

4

JOHN WOKE UP the morning of December 24th, completely exhausted. You couldn't even really call it waking up, because he'd barely slept.

It had taken every bit of control he had not to give Miss Priss next door a piece of his mind. That, or head for Minky's Tavern, a place he hadn't visited in years. He'd stormed home and cleaned the entire first floor with a violence that had the boys raising eyebrows and steering clear of him.

How dare she call him a charmer. She was rubbing salt in a wound he'd carried since childhood. He'd come from a long line of ne'er do well bad boys, not-to-be-trusted womanizers, right down to his own handsome, cheating dad. He didn't want to be that man.

But apparently, something about him still said Moretti, the no-good charmer.

He hated that her attitude could get to him. He was a new creation in Christ, right? So why did all the old baggage still pull him down?

He dragged himself out of bed at 8:00 and walked into the communal bathroom, since the bathroom in his apartment was torn up, waiting for him to get the time to fix the linoleum. Unlike usual, every towel was neatly hung up and every surface sparkled. Last night it had been a mess—his own cleaning frenzy had petered out before he'd gotten upstairs—so one of the boys must have done it.

Zeke, the oldest, probably got the credit for the cleanup. He'd come from a wealthy home out west, and even though his parents were a disaster morally, he'd taken care of his younger brother and knew what a clean house was supposed to look like.

He was easily the most mature of the four boys, with a judgmental streak a mile wide. Now that he was back on the right path, he took a fatherly attitude toward the other boys that made John smile. Shoot, maybe he'd forced one of the other boys to clean. That would be something else. Zeke was going places, no doubt.

A hot shower improved John's mood enough that he managed to put on a Christmas sweater someone had given him —yeah, he was that guy—and headed downstairs. Surprise, surprise, someone had even fixed coffee. He tasted it—way too strong, but that was better than weak—and poured cereal into a bowl.

Like magic, Zeke appeared in the kitchen. "You seemed pretty mad last night."

"Yep." John scanned the newspaper headlines.

"How come?"

John studied the eighteen-year-old ruefully. It was pretty bad when a kid was the one trying to draw out the adult. "Annie got to me," he admitted. "Called me some things I didn't like, and accused you boys of taking her granny's doll from the nativity scene." He wouldn't have said as much to the younger boys, worrying they'd retaliate against her, but Zeke had developed good sense and self-control in the year-and-a-half he'd been at Covenant School.

"What'd she call you?" Zeke asked.

He waved a hand. "Doesn't matter. The point is, she's going to call the police if we don't get that doll back. And you know as well as I do that police involvement is the last thing any of you guys need."

"For real." Zeke studied his nails. "I was serious when I said we wouldn't steal it. Only..."

"Only what?"

"Only, I'm not sure I'm speaking for everyone."

"What did you hear? Because we can't let this get to the police level."

"I didn't hear anything, but I just...I think we have to figure it out."

"Yeah, well, give me some ideas about how," John said, "because I'm out of patience. Old Miss Clara is the last person to take out your mad on."

When Zeke started to protest, John held up a hand. "I believe you when you say you didn't do it, but like you, I'm not too sure about the others." He didn't want to outright accuse Rock—he knew well enough the pain of being questioned because of your appearance and background—but he suspected that was where the fault lay.

Zeke shrugged. "Just don't push too hard, or you'll never get it back."

"And I want to. That doll belonged to Miss Clara's daughter who died. Annie's mother. So there's a sentimental value."

"Wow." Zeke nodded like he got that, even though John knew for a fact that Zeke's own mother was a wealthy, shallow person who was only tolerable when you compared her to Zeke's horrible father. But somewhere, Zeke had picked up some empathy, and he was smart as a whip. "What are you gonna do?"

The idea came to John full blown and he went with it, knowing he had to trust his instincts on this one. "We're going to make nice and make up. All of us."

TWO HOURS LATER, the five of them were taking turns dragging a massive Christmas tree toward Miss Clara's. Complaints rang out continually, like off-key Christmas bells.

"Man, she ain't gonna have decorations for this big of a tree."

"We must be crazy."

"I got scratched, man!"

"This sucks."

A few people were out on decorated porches, smoking or watching the spectacle; a few other pedestrians came and went from the diner on the corner, the small shop-mart, or the liquor store. A few catcalled the boys.

Zeke and Rock both ignored the mild harassment, stoically carrying the tree. But when John told the other two to take another turn, it wasn't three minutes until Boone dropped his end with a curse. "I ain't doing this, man. It's not my fault somebody done ripped off the old lady's baby doll."

"Me either." Daniel, who tended to do whatever the other boys did, threw down his end of the tree. "Why should we drag this all the way from one end of town to the other?"

They were right outside Jefferson's Diner, so John leaned the tree up against the side of the building himself. "Come on in, we'll get a burger. I've got some stuff to say to you boys."

"Great, now you done it," Rock grumbled, but they all trooped inside. Owner and cook Jeff Jefferson was known for his thick, greasy, delicious cheeseburgers, and the boys didn't get them often.

Once they were at the table, waiting for their food, John dove in. "Look," he said, "even if Miss Clara's place hadn't been vandalized, we should help our neighbors. That's what the Bible says, and that's what we should do."

"Ain't nobody ever helped me," Boone grumbled. Boone had come to them from Florida, where a compassionate judge had seen the intelligence behind the swagger in this beat-up kid from a brawling alcoholic family. Boone was completely resistant to the gospel, and John took it there'd been some conflict between his family and the church people back home. Well, John wouldn't push it, but he'd gotten a bible into Boone's hands and gotten the boy to attend a few church services. The rest was work for the good Lord to do.

"That's not true, that nobody ever helped you," Zeke pointed out. "John's helping you right now, giving you a place to stay. He doesn't have to be here with us at Christmas, but he's doing it."

"Yeah," Rock said, "cuz he's got no life."

Daniel high-fived him. "You got that right."

"Why *are* you doing this, man?" Boone asked him.

The tables had been turned on him, and John didn't much like it. Generally, he counted on the selfishness of teenagers to keep from having to share too much about himself. But now, four pairs of eyes were looking at him, and whether their interest was genuine, or stemmed from their desire to avoid more lecturing, he figured he had to answer. Honesty was the key to keeping these boys' fragile trust. "I'm here because I'm the only staffer without a family. Everyone else had somewhere to go."

"Yeah, but why don't you have anyone? Why didn't you get married? Ladies are crazy about you."

"He's a player!" Handsome Daniel shook his head in disbelief. "Phone's always blowing up."

"Yeah. And it's weird, because it's not like you're that good looking." Rock, who was more rugged than pretty and knew it, looked genuinely curious.

John chuckled. "I'd never win a beauty contest, that's for sure. But women aren't as superficial as we men are. If you treat 'em right and try to be a good person, you don't have to look like a movie star."

"Yeah," Rock said, punching Daniel in the arm.

"So where'd you screw up?" Boone was frowning, like he was trying to make what John was saying match with his own background. "'Cause I don't see any fine ladies on your arm right now."

"Good point." John had to restrain himself from ruffling the kid's hair. No touching ever, not at this age, not for these kids. "Problem is," he added, thinking it through as he spoke, "I meet a lot of women who're out to have fun. But I don't seem to click with the marrying kind."

"Maybe it's you, not them." Zeke looked thoughtful.

John pointed a finger at him. "Hey, watch it. You're getting too smart."

"Better to be single," Daniel advised with all the confidence of a seventeen-year-old ladies' man.

"I don't know," John admitted. "Do you

want to grow up and spend holidays alone, or with a bunch of smart-alecks like you?"

The question struck all of them, and there was a little silence around the table. John took advantage of it. "Look, you guys are young and strong and you've got everything going for you. Your whole lives ahead of you. Those are real assets, and you've got to figure out what to use them for."

"Use 'em to keep on top of other people," Rock suggested.

"No. No. Use them in service to others. We're here to help our neighbors. Giving is living."

"You sound like a pastor."

"I'm anything but. I've made more mistakes than you guys have even thought of."

Their food arrived, juicy and good-smelling. Talk stopped, and they all dug in.

"You guys have practice for Christmas Eve service later this afternoon," John reminded them, "so let's move."

He didn't know whether it was the conversation or the food, but when they left the restaurant, the boys had renewed energy to pull the Christmas tree to Miss Clara's doorstep.

They looked at John and he looked at the door.

And he realized that he was going to have to confront Annie again. The thought churned his stomach. Reluctantly, he climbed the steps and knocked at the door. Knocked again.

No answer.

"They ain't here,' Rock said, sounding relieved. "We'll just leave it and go."

"They gotta be here. Where would they go?" Zeke climbed the steps and pounded the door again.

High-pitched barking sounded from deep in the big house, then closer to the door. "Coming, coming" came a shout from inside.

The door opened to reveal Annie, wearing a down vest and hat, with a streak of dirt across her face. Behind her, Miss Clara's face peered out anxiously from a hooded winter coat. Even the dog shivered in a ridiculous red coat.

"You guys playing Arctic Circle?" John asked. "What's wrong?"

"It's the furnace. It's out, and I can't get anyone to come repair it on Christmas Eve."

"And we're about freezing to death in here, but we'll survive," Miss Clara said cheerfully. "Come on in, all of you."

"Um…you want me to take a look?" He nodded at the boys to put down the tree, which the two women were obviously too frazzled to deal with right now.

"That would be wonderful."

"Not saying I can do much. Mind if the boys come downstairs with me and learn something about furnace repair?"

"We're fine, we don't need to." Rock, Zeke, and Daniel were all shaking their heads. Only Boone looked interested; though the troubled kid from Florida hid it well, he was practically a genius at science and was fascinated with how things worked.

And John was never one to pass up a learning opportunity for his boys. "Come on, all of you. You never know when you might need to know this."

"I'll fix hot chocolate." Miss Clara sounded happy.

So they all trooped downstairs after Annie, including the little dog, who jumped ecstatically at the boys. The basement was unfinished, and the furnace a behemoth.

John studied it from all different angles, talking it through with the boys and Annie, trying to figure out what was wrong.

Forty-five minutes later, he admitted defeat. "You need to replace a couple of gas valves and maybe a burner. And there's nowhere that will deliver those on Christmas Eve. There are emergency repair people, but they cost a lot. Better if you can go stay with relatives."

Annie was sitting cross-legged on the floor, the dog asleep in her lap. "Trouble is, we don't have relatives in town to stay with. I guess we'll check into a hotel. I have to get Grandma out of here, she's freezing."

John frowned. He knew what he ought to offer to do. What he wanted to do. But he just didn't dare.

"You know," Zeke said, "we have plenty of room over at the school."

"Yeah," Daniel added, "youth and strength ought to help out need and age." He cast a snarky smile in John's direction, but it wasn't all snark. Spiritually, Daniel was a seeker. He didn't resist John's evangelical efforts, and they'd had a few good conversations. That was fine.

John had the feeling Daniel would come around.

"We couldn't possibly—" Annie's eyes had gone wide.

"You should come, Ma'am. It's Christmas Eve, after all." Boone turned toward the stairs. "I'll tell Miss Clara to get ready."

"But what about the Christmas tree?" Daniel asked. "We brought you and Miss Clara a tree."

"You brought us a tree?" Annie said weakly.

"Yeah," John said. "It's outside. But we'd..." He swallowed to compensate for the sudden dryness of his throat. "We'd love to have you come spend Christmas with us. We can set up the tree over there. I can cook." God help him, was that happiness he was feeling? Happiness at having a woman—two women, one young and gorgeous and another old and gorgeous as well, in her own way—in his home? "What do you think?"

"But we'd have to bring Macy. Don't you have a cat?"

"The cat will keep Macy in his place." He picked up the shivering little dog. "Come on, buddy. Time to make a couple of new friends."

5

ANNIE CAST UP a prayer to the God she didn't pay near enough attention to. What was she going to do? Poor Gran couldn't freeze for the next day-and-a-half. But to spend the holiday with a bunch of hoodlums of the sort she was terrified of, the sort who'd broken her family, struck fear, plain and simple, into her heart. "I don't think we'd better. We don't want to impose."

"Miss Clara's packing," Boone called down the stairs.

Annie drew in a deep breath and looked at John. He was smiling at her, one eyebrow quirked.

Her breathing quickened. Which wasn't good.

"You'll have your own rooms, both of you," he said. "With locks on the doors."

Had he read her mind?

"I do a big seafood dinner on Christmas Eve." He actually winked at her. "Feast of the Seven Fishes. It's an Italian thing."

Annie's heart caught. He was persuading her with all his masculine charm...to let him do a favor for her and Gran. Who *was* this guy?

"His seafood's good," Zeke said. "It's why I stay for Christmas."

"That's bull," Rock said. "You got nowhere else to go. None of us do."

All of a sudden, Annie got her mind off herself. It couldn't be easy for these boys to be away from their families at Christmas. Maybe some of them didn't even have families. And maybe—*duh, genius*—that was why they acted out.

And if having a grandma figure there in the house helped them feel at home...if maybe even she, the woman who'd never had a good relationship and never wanted kids...if she could do something to help them get through the holiday in a happy way, then wasn't it her Christian duty to do so?

And then there was John and his smile. "All right," she said. "Thank you very much for the offer. We accept."

~

AN HOUR later they'd moved their overnight bags to the big building next door. Macy had chased Whiskers through the hallways for a few minutes, and then his hysterical barking had stopped abruptly. He'd trotted back to them with his tail between his legs and was now sulking, nose on paws, on a blanket in a corner of the lounge.

Gran had put her things in one of the downstairs dorm rooms and, from the raucous sounds of it, was helping the boys decorate the giant Christmas tree they'd dragged into the common lounge.

John opened the door to an upstairs dorm room adjacent to his apartment. Neat and plain, it was clearly meant for a male student, but hey, she couldn't complain—it was blessedly warm in here. The single bed, covered with a thick navy-blue quilt, looked comfortable, and there was a dresser, desk, and nightstand.

She walked over to the only picture on the wall and studied it. "Is this you?"

"Yeah." He came over and stood beside her. "I had this room when I first moved here, before I fixed up the apartment. Never got around to transferring the non-essentials."

She was still examining the photo of a younger John in Army fatigues, surrounded by a half-dozen waist-high, dark-haired kids. "Where was this taken?"

He squinted at the photo and then stepped back. "Outside Beirut, I think. Forgot that was in here."

"You like kids." It was a statement, not a question.

He laughed. "Guess I do. The more down and out, the better. Those were some street kids I kinda befriended."

She met his eyes. "How come?"

"How come what? I like the ragged ones?"

She nodded.

He lifted a shoulder, color rising in his face. "I was a street kid myself, sort of. Never had a lot of opportunities, but there were a few adults that helped me along the way and I remembered what a difference they made."

"Never had any of your own?"

He hesitated, then shook his head. "No. I wasn't blessed that way." He gestured at the drawers, pulled one open. "Make yourself at home."

"We're only staying a day. Wait, what's in there?"

"Two days, probably, because you won't be able to get anyone out here until the day after Christmas." He shut the dresser drawer and opened the one below it. "Use this one."

"Okay." But as soon as he stepped away from the dresser, she opened the top drawer back up. "Whose medals are these?"

"They're mine. Look, I'm gonna go downstairs and see what help they need with the tree."

"Why are they hidden away? Aren't you proud of them?"

He shrugged. "Most of 'em, everyone who served overseas got. Making it home might be something to thank God for, but it's not something to brag about."

She lifted one, a gold star on a red, white

and blue ribbon. "The Silver Star's nothing to brag about?"

"You recognize it?"

Her eyes widened. "Not only do I recognize it, I have total respect for it. You must've risked your life, stood out above everyone else in your unit. Extraordinary acts of bravery." She stroked the medal with one finger. "I had an uncle who was awarded one of these, only it was posthumous."

"Yeah." He rubbed the back of his neck. "There was too much of that. It doesn't seem right to... I made it home. That's enough."

She looked into his eyes, sad eyes that had maybe seen too much. "I appreciate what you did for our country. And I think you should display it with pride, *be* proud."

"I'm gonna go help out the boys. You come down when you're ready."

After he left, Annie stood looking at the medals and the photo, thinking about the modest man she was just starting to get to know. John hadn't had an easy life, from the looks of things, and he didn't have a family with whom to spend Christmas. But he was helping kids who needed it in the worst way. The fact that he was a genuine military hero went to show what he was like—he wouldn't hesitate in sacrificing himself for others.

Just being around him made her want to be a better person. Because what was she doing, really, with her life? Like him, she'd never had kids, but she didn't do anything to help other people's kids, aside from donating a little money here and there. Her job, helping rich people get richer, kept her too busy to even have a dog or a cat.

John was a good neighbor to her grandma, a good father figure to these boys, and she...she was an advertising executive with a beachfront Florida condo that was almost always empty, because she was almost always working.

Nosy, she opened the other drawers in the dresser, but they were empty. When she opened the drawer in the nightstand, she found a Bible.

She almost closed the drawer again, but on impulse, she opened the Bible and her eyes widened. So much writing, so much highlighting. Little cryptic notes in the margins.

She looked at the front of the book and

saw the inscription: *John Moretti, Grade Twelve.*

Interesting. So his religion wasn't only an outward show.

Could you be religious, really religious on the inside, and also as sexy and fun-loving as John?

The direction of her own thoughts flustered her, and she put the Bible back into the drawer, shoved her suitcase into a corner, and headed downstairs to help with the Christmas decorating.

~

THAT EVENING, John blew out the candles on the dinner table with a feeling that was a lot like nervousness. Where did he get off thinking he had the right to the warm home and family life he'd gotten a taste of tonight?

Not when he'd spoiled all his chances with the woman he loved and left her to seek consolation in the arms of another man. That reality had kept him from forming a deep, loving, Godly relationship in all the years after. He just wasn't worthy.

But seeing Annie's hesitant efforts to befriend the boys, her genuine care of her grandma, and hearing her grandma brag about Annie's incredible success in the business world, he had a serious case of admiration.

And now, he was all but alone in the house with her.

They had a couple of hours until midnight mass. The priest had stopped by to take the boys to the youth rehearsal, so for once, there weren't a bunch of teens underfoot.

Miss Clara had pleaded age as an excuse for not going to midnight mass. "Jesus knows I'm loyal and I'm celebrating his birth, but I'm eighty-nine years old and I've earned the right to take a pass on services when I need to." She'd hugged everyone and gone to her bedroom, firmly shutting the door.

John cleared the last of the dishes and headed into the kitchen, where Annie was scrubbing a large, greasy pan.

"You don't have to do that," he protested, coming up behind her. "Let's leave it to soak."

"It'll only take a minute," she said, smiling at him over her shoulder. "You did all the cooking and it was a great meal. Let me at least help with cleanup. Sit down."

"Are you this bossy to your employees?"

"Bossier." She smiled, then bit her lip.

"Missing work?"

"More like *not* missing it. I haven't taken a vacation in a long time, haven't really gotten away. But the agency is closed over Christmas, so no emails, no tweets, no phone calls. It feels really good to slow down and relax."

"We have a slower way of life here than in Miami," he said, taking the pan from her to dry. "Pittsburgh's bad weather can force you to relax, force people to come together."

"Like this." She gestured around them. "Who'd have thought I would be spending Christmas Eve at the Covenant School? I don't even approve of it!"

"Why don't you?" he asked. "I mean, aside from the fear of delinquents stealing from your Gran. Because honestly, if you were that afraid for her safety, you'd have gotten her out of this neighborhood ten years ago."

"Believe me, I tried. She's never been willing to go." She sighed. "I know it's crazy, but I remember what gangs of kids can be like."

"To the point where you can't stand teens even now?" He looked skeptical.

She bit her lip. "It sounds neurotic, doesn't it? But it's because of..." She broke off.

"Go ahead," he encouraged her.

She met his eyes and he couldn't believe the pain he saw there. *Ouch.* That was raw. That was real.

She opened her mouth to speak, closed it, swallowed hard. "I have...I *had*...a sister."

6

JOHN HAD THE feeling that he was inches away from unlocking the real Annie. "Come on," he said, tugging her hand. "Let's go sit down. Can I pour you some coffee? Cup of tea?"

She took tea, and five minutes later they were sitting at opposite corners of the couch in front of the fire. The twinkling lights of the Christmas tree provided the only other light in the room.

He poked her gently with his sock-covered foot. "Tell me about your sister."

She drew in a shaky breath, let it out slowly. "You sure you want to hear? It's not a very uplifting story."

"If it explains a little bit more about you, I want to hear it." Maybe it would give him some insight into why she acted the way she did around the boys.

And the Lord help him, but he wanted her to get over her problems with the kids he considered his own. That was the only way they could ever have a chance at a relationship. A pretty slim chance, considering that she lived in Florida, but it was something.

"Rhonda had some cognitive delays," she said in a voice so soft he had to lean forward to hear it. "She was always in special classes. But she was a sweetheart. Never met a stranger."

"Older than you or younger?"

"My twin."

"Oh. Wow." He reached forward, gripped her foot in his hand, and started a gentle massage.

"Anyway, we went through high school together. She stayed a couple years longer, in those transition classes, you know? Learning to function in the real world." She laughed softly. "She never got real good at it, but she tried hard."

"You lived with your mom then? Or your grandma?"

"Both. We'd moved in with Gran when we were little, and she raised us just as much as Mom did. More, really, because Mom worked a lot." She scrunched her face. "You sure you want to hear the rest of this?"

"Tell me." He kept rubbing her feet.

"Okay. So after she finally was done with school and in a work program, she wanted to move out, be independent, feel like an adult. So we were making plans for that. Or, I should say, Mom and Gran were. I was busy with college. Living at home, but spending all my time working and going to school and, you know, partying."

"Makes sense, at that age."

"Yeah. Well, Rhonda wanted to do that stuff too, I guess. She met some people in a halfway house and they became her best friends, or at least, she thought so."

John didn't have a good feeling about this. "What kind of halfway house?"

"People who were just getting out of prison. Or juvie. Rehabilitated, supposedly." Her mouth twisted and she shut her eyes, then opened them. "There were four of them that lived in a big house, just a couple blocks over. Four, and…" She swallowed hard. "And a live-in supervisor."

"Your mother and grandmother let her be friends with them?"

"Mom and Gran didn't know what kind of people they were." She shook her head hard. "They were doing what they saw fit, letting her make some choices. She was twenty years old, a legal adult, and she wasn't…she wasn't terribly impaired, you understand. She had a low IQ, but she could learn. She was like a permanent ten-year-old, maybe even twelve. And she had a great heart and emotional wisdom. She thought these people needed her." She almost choked on the words.

"Of course. It's got to be hard to know where to draw that line."

"Yeah." She pulled a fleece blanket off the back of the couch and wrapped it around herself protectively. Leaving her feet free so he could keep massaging them. Even through the socks, he could tell that she had nice feet. Small and shapely. Pretty, just like her.

He wanted to spare her telling this story,

because he could imagine the ending it was going to have. Something awful must have happened to her twin, and if that was the case, it explained a lot about the high-strung, uptight side of Annie.

She was still looking into the fire. "I…I knew those people, too."

He stiffened at her change in tone. "What were they like?"

She shrugged. "They weren't the types I would have chosen as friends. One guy, the ringleader, bragged a lot about himself. The rest of them were followers, mostly doing whatever the leader, Tom, said to do."

"How'd you know them? Did you visit there too?"

"A little," she said. "I actually…I actually knew the supervisor."

He nodded.

"They drank too much, and smoked, and partied, but hey, didn't we all, back in those days?"

He nodded ruefully. "I sure did."

"Me, too. So there weren't any red flags. At least, not that I caught." She stared into the fire, her eyes looking a little bit shiny. "You don't know how much I wish I'd been more careful, more discerning. I was so caught up in myself and my friends and my activities. Maybe if I'd have spent more time with Rhonda..." She trailed off, biting her lip. A tear ran down her cheek.

"Hey. We were all selfish back at that age. Most twenty-year-olds are." He leaned forward, thumbed the tear off her cheek.

She pulled back, took a deep breath, and squared her jaw. "So. The group got into a big fight at a certain point. In fact, it was right around this time of year."

"Your gran said you have a hard time with Christmas."

Annie looked surprised. "I guess I do. Anyway, one of the girls thought Rhonda was after Tom, who was this girl's boyfriend. She started, and I quote, 'punishing' Rhonda. And it went downhill from there."

"Meaning?" John had a sinking feeling.

"Meaning they tormented her for a couple of days before they finally killed her."

John's stomach clenched right along with his fists. He'd seen a lot and heard more, but the idea of someone torturing and killing a disabled girl was about the worst.

"Whether they killed her on purpose or

accidentally, I don't know," she went on in a flat, toneless voice. "And then two of the guys wrapped her body in garbage bags and carried it to the dumpster outside the municipal building and threw her inside."

"Oh, Annie." He moved her legs to the side and scooted close to her so he could fold her into his arms. "I'm so sorry. That's terrible." He paused, then asked, "Did they ever bring those people to justice?"

She nodded. "Yes. Three of them got fifty-to-life. And Tommy is on death row."

He shut his eyes against the pain. "So you had to go through a trial?"

"All separate ones. It went on for a couple of years." She looked at him. "It's long over, but I...I never have gotten over it. Maybe I never will."

"Oh, honey." He held her close and she let out a few muffled sobs. She didn't lose control, though; she was one of the most controlled women he'd ever met.

After a minute she scooted out of his arms, got up, and grabbed a tissue from a box on the end table. She blew her nose and dabbed at her eyes. "So you see, I'm a little... screwed up. And I don't like anything like a halfway house. That's why I had so many objections to the Covenant School."

It all made sense now—her animosity toward the school, her fears when the boys approached her. After the trauma she'd faced, John couldn't blame her. "Your gran didn't feel the same way?"

She shook her head. "Gran is an incredible woman. She forgave. She even visited Tommy in prison for a while, until it got to be too much for her."

"And your mom?"

"Mom…fell apart. She blamed herself. Got hooked on narcotics, painkillers and stuff like that, got in a car accident while stoned out of her mind, and that was that."

John clenched his jaw against what he wanted to say—that her mother had another daughter to whom she had a responsibility. And she'd abdicated it. Leaving Annie to face her grief alone.

He wanted to hold her, to comfort her, but she was sitting stiff and rigid and she looked as untouchable as an ice sculpture.

"So how has this all affected you? I can hardly imagine what that would be like. Your twin."

She met his eyes. "It's...it's kind of broken me. And I don't know how to put the pieces back together."

He reached out and clasped her hand, needing to make contact even though nothing about her invited touch. "Did you get counseling?"

She nodded. "We all did. Me most of all. Mom couldn't deal with it, and she chose another way out. Gran did a little counseling with me, and a little on her own, but she has her faith. That's what got her through."

"What about you? What about your faith?"

She shook her head. "I can't understand why God let that happen to Rhonda. Rhonda was a believer. She was so goodhearted and loving. She never did a bad thing on purpose in her whole life."

John looked at the Christmas tree's twinkling lights. He'd thought through the problem of pain and suffering in the world and what it meant about God, and he'd come to an understanding that made sense to him. But now wasn't the time for a sermon. "I'm not surprised such an awful experience affected your faith. How could it not?"

"It ruined it. I can't forgive God."

He closed his eyes for a minute and then opened them again, scooted closer to her, and looked right into her eyes. "Annie. I get how you feel that way, for sure. But I also don't know how you could get through something like that without God's help."

"He didn't help Rhonda," she said, turning her face away.

"You don't know that. Maybe he did." He squeezed her cold hands, rubbed them. "And you can bet that he's loving her now. I believe that with my whole heart."

She shrugged. "I can't. That's all, I just can't."

She was such a sad person. And this explained everything about her—why she was cold and standoffish, why she didn't like his boys or the school, why she was so closed off and uptight.

And he had the feeling that gentle talk wasn't what would get through to her, and God forgive him, but he wanted to get through. Wanted to wake her up. Wanted to see who she was when this cloak of grief came off.

"So," he said, "how's that working for you?"

Her eyes widened. "How's what working?"

"Being angry. Hating God. Closing yourself off from other people."

"I have lots of friends!" She got up, walked over to the little dog sleeping in the corner, picked him up, and carried him back to the couch. She petted him with intensity, pointedly ignoring John.

He waited until she finally looked at him and nodded. "But you're not at one of your friends' houses. You're here with me."

"I have Gran to take care of!"

"Right. And that's a good thing. But friends are good, too."

Whiskers walked by slowly, seeming to swagger in front of the dog, who tensed and growled.

"Anyway, Mr. Perfect, I don't see you having a lot of places to go on Christmas. I hear you spend a lot of time talking to your cat."

"Did the boys tell you that?" He reached down and scooped up Whiskers, who protested with a mild yowl. "You've got a point. I'm not the best at relationships, for sure. And I don't have as good of a reason as you do."

She'd been puffed up to keep arguing, but at his soft words, she deflated. "I've never been in a relationship, not a real one."

He cocked his head to one side, studying her. "Are you serious? A woman as pretty as you are?"

"I've always dated men who weren't really available. I've never been married. Never had kids." Now, tears were rolling down her cheeks. "I don't think I can, John. I hate it, but I can't really love anyone. I can't trust people. And I'm just so angry!"

He wanted to help her, *really* wanted to, but he felt out of his league here. "You said you've had counseling?"

She nodded, looking impatient. "Yes, at the time and then twice after. Trying to fix myself, trying to heal. I don't want to be like this, but I can't get out of it!"

He didn't know what to do or how to do it, but he went with his gut and plunged ahead. "You know, God can do what man alone can't."

"I told you, I don't trust God!"

"Have you tried? Have you prayed?"

"I can't pray. Stop it!"

"I'm not stopping," he said urgently, "Because you're worth it, Annie. You're worth saving. You deserve a life, and love, and God loves you. Just like he loved Rhonda. And just like he loves that man on death row. Nobody's unredeemable, Annie."

"Oh, yes they are. Tommy Smitherton is unredeemable. And I can't help it, I'm not going to forgive him. Not ever. So I can't be a real Christian."

"Yes, you can!" He took her hands and squeezed them and got close, trying not to be distracted by how pretty she was, by the smell of her hair and the urgent rise and fall of her chest. "God takes us where we are, even if that's a really terrible place. He's at home with sinners. He hung out with the tax collectors and prostitutes. He can help you get a fresh start."

She stared down at her jean-clad legs, her mouth twisting.

"You just have to stop resisting him and embrace what he has to offer."

She shook her head rapidly. "I'm not going to do that."

He squeezed her hands. “I’m rooting for you to change your mind.”

“But until then,” she said, “you probably don’t want anything to do with me. Right? Because no one likes a cranky, bitter woman of a certain age.”

He looked into her teary, pretty eyes. He did have his concerns, but he also had confidence in the miracles God could work. And he could see that she was hurting and that she needed, above all else, acceptance and reassurance.

And then, because he was only a man, with a man’s desires and weaknesses and foolishness, he did the only thing he could think to do.

He kissed her.

7

ANNIE'S HEART ALREADY felt shredded, and she was worn out from the emotional storm. So when John leaned forward and pressed his lips to hers, she let her arms circle his neck without a second thought.

It had been a long time since a man had kissed her. A long time since she'd wanted to be kissed. And his firm-but-gentle lips on hers, the way he didn't let go, the way he cupped her face as if she were precious, that was new to her.

He pulled back after a minute, tucked a piece of her hair behind her ear. "You're really something, you know that?"

"Some kind of a mess, and now you know that," she said with an uneasy laugh. Because John didn't know quite all of it. He didn't know her own role in the situation. But she didn't know if she could tell him that, because then he really wouldn't like her much.

"Some kind of beautiful. And sexy. And lovable." He leaned forward and kissed her again.

His tongue came into play this time and suddenly, it wasn't a comforting kiss anymore. It was passion, controlled for sure, but she felt a warming inside that she hadn't felt in a really long time. Maybe ever, not like this. She opened to him, let him take her with his mouth, let him sweep her away. A little sound came from her throat, involuntarily, evoking a sexy growl from him.

She touched his face, feeling the heavy stubble there. Tangled her fingers in his hair. And she felt. Felt like she hadn't felt in years, hadn't let herself feel since Rhonda.

The panic that always accompanied that attracted feeling nudged at her, but the good clean manliness of him swept through her forcefully, plowing away her guilt and her fears. She tipped her head back and let him play, and when he started to pull away, she murmured and held on.

He chuckled a little against her mouth. "Now, now. We gotta behave."

"But that's no fun." She couldn't believe that was her speaking in that low, throaty voice.

He gave her lower lip a tiny nip that sent heat all the way to her toes, and then backed off, cradling her face again like he had at first. "You're a surprising lady."

"Is that good or bad?" she murmured.

He crinkled his eyes at her and half-frowned. "I'm not sure I'm ready for surprises at my age."

"You don't kiss like an old man."

His eyebrows shot up and Annie blushed to the edges of her hair. What on earth was she thinking? But she hadn't felt this alive in years, and she didn't want the feeling to end.

Still, she knew she wasn't going to let this attraction head to a natural conclusion. That didn't fit her values, and anyway, her old guilt wouldn't allow her to get even close to a real connection. So they wouldn't have a relationship, physical or otherwise, but she couldn't help wanting to pretend.

An idea struck her. "I need to go get something at home. I forgot to bring anything to wear to church tonight." That way, she could help ease them out of the temptation this romantic, dimly lit room offered... and also find something really pretty to wear. All of a sudden, church felt like a date. And for once, she really wanted to go.

"Okay," he said, "I'll walk you over."

"Would you? That will be great."

JOHN CROOKED his arm for Annie to take as they made their way over the icy sidewalk to Miss Clara's house. He didn't know what to feel.

Had he taken advantage of her by kissing her? Especially when he knew he wasn't going to be able to follow through?

Maybe you could, a voice said inside. But another, stronger voice argued back. *No way, you're not good enough for her*. It was a voice from his past on the street, a voice from his guilt at the losses of his military time in Beirut and Grenada, a voice from his past love, who he'd never fully let go of, even though he'd never been enough for her either.

Since the situation with Emily had gone south, he'd pretty much confined himself to no-strings relationships with women he didn't have to worry about.

Annie was different. He had enormous respect for all she'd accomplished in her work and all she'd overcome in her personal life. He no longer judged her for not spending much time in Pittsburgh, because he understood how painful this place must be for her.

And it wasn't just respect, it was attraction. Annie was one of the most beautiful women he'd ever seen, and when the tense lines of her face softened, when she relaxed into wanting and desire, she was simply a knockout.

The trouble was, she was way, way out of his league.

What would a woman like Annie want with a guy who'd gone into the Marines instead of college because he'd had no money? Who'd then struggled through the only state university that would take him, who'd become a low-paid, inner-city shop teacher, and then had put all his savings into an ancient school and lived from month to month?

Annie was a thoroughbred while he was a workhorse. She should be matched up with some executive who wore a suit each day.

"You're quiet," she said now as they approached her grandmother's house. "You okay?"

"Yeah." The last thing he wanted was for her to worry. "Just thinking about things. Feeling lucky you're walking down the street with me." That much was true. He had to be the luckiest man in Pittsburgh to be getting this kind of attention from a woman like Annie.

"I'm going to run upstairs for a couple minutes," she said.

"I'll be down here. Take your time." Doubts assailed him. Who knew, maybe she needed to call a boyfriend back in Florida.

He wandered downstairs to take another look at her furnace. Turned on the lights and shone a flashlight around the big old metal monster. Tapped on a few parts. Twisted things around, loosened what was tight and tightened what was loose.

He wasn't so focused on fixing it now, just trying to kill some time by doing something constructive with his hands. But when he heard the motor shift, he got focused. He'd always been good with motors.

He knelt down and slid underneath and worked with that tricky valve and the burner that had been clogged. Studying everything, he wasn't even sure how much time had passed.

Finally, he was rewarded with a rumbling sound. The furnace was about to come on, at least, he hoped so.

He brushed his hands on the sides of his jeans and trotted up the stairs.

He arrived in the hallway just in time to see Annie coming down from the top floor.

She wore a dark red velvet dress that swirled around her legs, and high heeled boots, black and sexy. She looked amazing. And here he was, dirty and grubby in his old clothes, not in any sense a match for her.

He stood admiring her and feeling his own unworthiness, kicking himself for kissing her. Wanting to compliment her, but what came out of his mouth instead, probably out of a desire to impress her, were plain, everyday words. "I fixed your furnace."

Annie stopped dead still at the bottom of the staircase, staring at John as the pieces clicked into place.

He'd kissed her, and she'd thought it meant something. But now, he'd come over here and fixed her furnace so that she and Gran could go back home.

She knew men tended to kiss and run, but John was doing it with breathtaking speed. He hadn't even noticed her new dress, the one she was wearing as a symbol of letting the bad stuff go, of reverting to her pre-trauma, carefree self.

She pressed her lips tight together and gave him a quick nod. Then she walked around checking the faucets and windows, making sure everything was tight. "It'll take a while for the house to warm up," she said finally, hearing the shrill, tense sound of her own voice. "Until then, is it okay if Gran stays at your place?"

"Of course. We'd like to have you stay

anyway, but it'll be nice to have a place to come home to, right?"

A place to come home to. Yeah.

She hadn't had that in years. This house used to be that to her, but since Rhonda's murder, Annie hadn't felt like this was home. Yet Florida never had become home to her, either. She'd furnished her condo with magazine-type décor, but it was as impersonal as a hotel room.

For just a minute there, she'd hoped that she could have a home here again. That healing was possible and that love was available, even to a thirty-five-year-old woman who'd never really loved in her life. That there were, in fact, second chances. Maybe even with God's help.

But the cruel joke was on her, because John obviously didn't want anything ongoing. Nothing lasting. He was pushing her away with both hands. Most likely he'd never even wanted them to stay at his place, but he was a decent guy, especially where Gran was concerned.

"So, you still want to go to church?" His voice sounded strange. "Because I'm going to have to clean up a little. Don't want someone mistaking me for a bum."

Did he want her to go to church with him? She couldn't tell and didn't know. "Well, I got this dress out," she said abruptly. "I need somewhere to wear it."

"Then come back with me while I change. We'll just have time to run down to the Cathedral before midnight." He reached out, touched the arm of her dress. "This is pretty."

"Thank you." She forced the words out past the walls she'd just hastily rebuilt around herself.

8

AN HOUR LATER they were at the midnight service at the cathedral. The place was amazing—huge, vaulted ceilings, stained glass spotlighted, evergreen garlands hanging and a couple of tall, lighted Christmas trees. The scent of pine and candles mingled together, catapulting Annie back to childhood holidays.

"You know, they were going to turn this place into a restaurant," John told her as they walked in. "But the neighborhood rose up to take it back."

"With your help, I'm guessing?" She was starting to realize how deeply John cared about this community.

He shrugged. "It's my old church, and I love coming here."

"That's cool. This place is packed."

They squeezed into a pew beside an older couple who obviously knew John. "You still directing that school?" the woman asked.

"Yeah." John shot Annie a quick glance and then leaned over to talk quietly with the couple.

What did they mean, directing the school? He was the maintenance man, wasn't he?

When he settled back in beside her, she called him on it. "What aren't you telling me? Are you in charge of the school?"

"I'm…the director, yeah."

"Why didn't you tell me?"

He cocked an eyebrow. "Why'd you assume I wasn't?"

She shrugged, trying to hide her embarrassment at her mistake. "Because I always saw you cutting the grass or shoveling sidewalks, fixing stuff."

He shrugged. "At a place like Covenant, everyone wears a lot of hats. I'm the maintenance man when the regular guy's off. I mentor all the boys, which means modeling hard work." He paused and then met her eyes. "Why? Does it make a difference?"

She sensed there was a lot riding on her answer, so she spoke carefully. "I'm actually impressed. I just wonder why you're hiding your light."

His dark eyebrows shot up. "Am I doing that?"

She smiled at him. "Looks like it from here. Medals in a drawer, acting like a janitor, pretending you don't have an education..."

"Don't dig too deep," he said, looking uncomfortable.

The organ started playing a blasting loud rendition of "O Come All Ye Faithful," and everyone stood up. The choir marched slowly toward the front of the church. Around her, hundreds of voices lifted in song.

She knew the words, all of them, didn't have to look at the screen on which the words were projected. It was like riding a bike; you never forgot the Christmas carols.

Beside her, John sang in a perfect, ringing baritone. He could easily be in the choir, could sing a solo. But of course, he didn't have time, given that he was also in charge of Covenant Academy.

And he wouldn't want to show off. She shook her head, biting back a smile. He was multitalented, obviously. But for all that, if you pushed past the confident surface, he seemed a little insecure.

Or did he just not want to reveal himself to *her*? She couldn't be sure, and her heart, which had opened a little with his kiss, locked tight again.

She sang along, and despite herself the music took her back to the same place the candles and evergreens had—to an earlier time before her family had gone so very wrong. She and her family had attended a different church, but of course, they'd sung this song. She remembered standing in a row with Rhonda, her mom, and Gran, singing joyously, so thrilled by the fact that they'd get to hold a lit candle at the end of the service. And then they'd go home and drink hot chocolate and open one present each.

It had been mixed up in her mind as a kid, the spiritual welcoming of the Christ child and the receiving of more mundane gifts. Probably it was like that for most kids. But Gran in particular had always stressed the spiritual. Had put out a nativity scene and had read to them from the Bible and had talked with wonder about the birth of Christ.

The choir was filing into the loft now, and a whole parade of kids, from little ones to teens, followed along and lined up in front of the church. And there, toward the back, were John's four. They were carrying a pallet on which a huge statue of Jesus rested.

She couldn't help remarking to John, "That looks heavy."

"They can carry a lot of weight if they work together."

The service, with its candle-lighting and scripture readings and hymn-singing, was beautiful, but gradually Annie lost her sense of ease. She felt somehow she was missing an opportunity. Maybe it was just that she wasn't a kid anymore, and she knew that people weren't to be trusted, and she didn't like knowing that the world wasn't as sweet and exciting as she'd found it when she was younger.

But when the preacher talked about humility and how the Christ child, the king of kings, had been born in a manger in a barn, she thought two things.

One, her Gran's Christ child was still missing. Would they ever find the baby doll?

And two, she hadn't known too many humble people in this crazy world.

Gran was one of them.

John was another. In fact, he was the most humble man she knew.

So maybe his not telling her about his position of power in the Covenant School had to do with humility. Maybe he didn't want to be liked for his position.

Maybe he was trying to live like Christ.

At the end of the service, the lights in the church were dimmed, and the pastor lit his own candle. The light spread from person to person throughout the church.

That was right, wasn't it? People were responsible for spreading the light of Christ.

When John lit her candle, he met her eyes. "Merry Christmas," he said.

Her breath almost stopped, looking into his eyes. It took a nudge from the neighbor on the other side before she thought to turn away and light the next candle.

Whatever the cost, she was falling for

John. Whatever the trust issues, she wanted to know him better, wanted to spend time with him, wanted to be a part of his life.

But how was that supposed to work, when she lived in Florida and he was rooted here? And when she wasn't comfortable with his neighborhood, his lifestyle, his boys?

And then the lights came up and the service was over and they crowded into the back of the church to collect the boys and tell them what a good job they'd done.

The boys even seemed a little moved by the service, and certainly, they were in a good mood.

"Are you eager to open your presents?" she asked them. She was going to try harder, try not to judge, try to make friends.

"Don't know that there are any presents under the tree," Zeke said to her in a matter-of-fact way. "We're not exactly a Christmas present crowd."

"Didn't you get each other anything? Or get anything for John?" As she said it, she realized that, of course, she hadn't gotten anything for any of the boys and certainly not for John. They'd gone from enemies to friends to, maybe more than friends in such a short time. She wanted to give him a gift, but what would that be?

He'd given her the gift of a listening ear, when she'd unburdened herself about Rhonda. Maybe there was something like that he needed, something intangible but heartfelt. She would hunt and see.

Meanwhile, though she didn't know much about teenagers, she figured that cash was always welcome. She'd wrap up a few dollars for each boy, and no doubt Gran would tuck some cookies and devotional cards into the stockings she'd seen hanging along the hearth.

They'd make themselves a Christmas one way or another.

JOHN WAS BEAT when they arrived home at 1 a.m., but he still had something to do. So he whipped up hot chocolate and gathered the boys around the kitchen table. Annie was still puttering around, wrapping presents and putting them under the tree. He was conscious of her. Even dressed in flannels and a T-shirt, she was a knockout. But a knockout who didn't trust him. He had to concentrate on his boys.

"So," he said to them once hot chocolate was served and they were all around the scarred pine table, "there *is* a Christmas present."

"I know, I know, it's a Bible!" Rock's tone held heavy sarcasm, but behind it, John heard the plaintive sound of a boy who'd never had the Christmas he'd hoped for. Part of Rock's problem was that he liked the good things in life and was angry he couldn't have them. John was hoping to set him up with a mentor, someone from the business community who could help him get some money-making skills so he'd go in the right direction. As a bonus, if Rock could hang out with a wealthier family, he might learn that being rich didn't equate to perfect happiness.

"No, I've already given you that. I do have a book, though." He got up, pulled a book from the top of the refrigerator, and set it in the middle of the table.

"What the—"

"Tattoos!"

"Lemme see!"

They all leaned over the tattoo notebook

John had borrowed, flipping through it, nudging one another out of the way.

"You're not really gonna get us tattoos, are you?" Zeke asked finally, looking at John.

"Randy Holzer is coming tomorrow and he's giving all four of you tattoos." John had thought of this weeks ago, had been debating it, but the events of the past few days had made up his mind and he'd gotten Randy, a tattoo artist who was single without much family in the area, to agree to come on Christmas afternoon.

"Anything we want?" Boone asked skeptically, his hand poised over an image of a bikini-clad lady on a motorcycle.

"No." He paused, making sure he had their attention. "You know I've been talking to you about using your youth and strength in service of other people, right?"

Zeke nodded and so did Daniel, but Boone and Rock looked skeptical.

"I want you to look through this book and agree together on a tattoo that says you'll do that forever. Make a pact, form a brotherhood. Agree to do good and help the weak." He stood up. "I'd like it if you prayed about it together, too. And I leave you to it. Don't go to bed until you've agreed on something, because Randy's coming to get started around two tomorrow."

He went out to the living room to make sure everything was locked up, and there was Annie still sitting on the couch. "You sure you know what you're doing with that?" she asked. "What if they choose a gang sign or something?"

"What if they choose a cross and do good in the world?" He sighed. He could see that her negative attitude was going to get in the way of their relationship, but there was no way he could think about that tonight. "Hey, thanks for coming to church tonight. I'm going to head up to bed."

She stood up, and looked so lost and lonely that John couldn't resist giving her a big hug. "Hey, buck up. It's not so bad. You'll get to go home to your Gran's tomorrow, and back to Florida real soon, I bet." Holding her felt great, and the idea of her leaving put a knife in his heart, but he had to be real. She was never going to accept him and what he believed in, what he was called to do.

With regret, he let her go.

9

AFTER A RESTLESS night dreaming of Grinches and mistletoe kisses, Annie woke to the sound of shouts. Young, male shouts. It shot her adrenaline up instantly, and she jumped out of bed, pulled a hoodie over her T-shirt and sweats, and ran downstairs. What could be wrong on Christmas morning?

The first person she encountered was John, on the landing between the first and second floors. He wore jeans and a white undershirt, his hair was mussed, and his heavily muscled chest looked utterly sexy and hot. But his face was white.

She put a hand on his arm. "What's wrong?"

"It's Rock. He's gone."

"Gone? On Christmas?"

The front door banged open, then shut, and cold air whisked through the house. "He's not outside, not nearby anyway," Zeke called upstairs.

"Come on," John said. "If you want." He squeezed her shoulder briefly, then turned and trotted downstairs.

Daniel emerged from the bathroom, gave her a blank look, and then followed John downstairs.

John whirled on him. "You share a room with Rock. You didn't hear anything, see anything?"

"I was out cold, man." Daniel shook his head.

"Think. Did he say anything that would hint at where he was going?"

"Not really. He...he didn't like the tattoo idea. But I didn't think he'd leave over it."

John uttered something that sounded suspiciously like a curse and grabbed his coat. "Lord, I want a drink."

"But you don't—" Boone looked worried.

"I said I wanted one, not that I'm having one. I'm gonna drive around a little, look for Rock. Zeke, come with me."

Annie had a moment of panic—John was leaving her here with two teenage boys she didn't know what to do with. But she was learning not to focus on herself in such a situation. "Come on," she said to the other two boys after John and Zeke had gone outside. "I'll fix you breakfast and we'll try to figure out what might have happened."

She cracked eggs and scrambled them, found a can of cinnamon rolls to bake. Gran came down, and they explained the situation to her over breakfast.

"I wonder why he didn't like the tattoo idea?" Annie mused. "It seems like a cool thing. What one did you decide on?"

Boone flipped through the book and pointed at a cross with a banner over it. "'Sacred Bond's gonna be written on either side."

"And what is your bond, young man?" Gran asked.

"We made a promise last night," Daniel said. "We're going to live our lives in the service of the weak and people who need protection. Like John does." He flushed, apparently embarrassed at having revealed so much.

"Did Rock promise?"

"Yeah, he did, but he wasn't happy about it. Had a bug up his..." He looked at the two women and blushed. "He seemed kinda down."

The old-fashioned black wall phone lit up, then gave a jarring ring.

Annie looked at the two boys and then realized that for all practical purposes, she was the adult n charge. She jumped up and grabbed the receiver.

"Is John there?" It was a boy's voice. A scared voice.

"No, he's not, but I can get a message to him. Is this Rock?"

Everyone at the table froze.

"Yeah. Listen...tell him I'm at the central police station and...I'm in trouble."

"We'll be right there. All of us," she said firmly. Then made sure she had the correct address, and rang off. "Call John," she ordered Daniel, "and tell him to meet us at the police station."

"But how are we gonna get there? John took the truck, right?"

Annie wrinkled her nose. "I guess...we're taking the Buick. Gran, you don't want to come, do you?"

"I should say so," she said emphatically. "I want to find out what they've done to that nice boy."

So they all piled into the Buick, which was a bear to drive, but Annie wasn't going to waste time waiting for a cab or for John to drive back to pick them up. Rock had sounded like a scared little boy. And no kid should be at the police station on Christmas. Unless he'd committed some awful crime, but she just couldn't believe that Rock had.

She drove as fast as she dared to the station in a mostly silent car, Gran beside her and the two boys in back. They pulled in just after John's truck did, and parked beside him, and John gave her a hurried sidearm hug. They all rushed inside together.

And there, slumped in a chair, was Rock.

Annie's heart went out to the boy. He had a swelling bruise on his face and his hand was wrapped in a makeshift bandage. He looked straight down at the floor.

John squatted in front of him. "You okay? What's going on?"

"He oughta be in juvie right now, only Chief had the Christmas spirit and said we had to wait till his guardian got here," grumbled a sour-looking police officer.

"What did he do wrong?"

"Let me count. One, he hung out on the street with a known drug dealer. Two, he was caught climbing a fence into a public housing project. Three, he refused to give up personal property when we brought him in."

"What personal property?" John asked.

Annie had to admire how he took the right tone, not kowtowing to the officers, but not defying them either.

"That's what was ridiculous. Some doll. Some really old doll that no one could possibly have—"

"Baby Jesus!" Annie and Gran cried out at the same time.

Both officers looked puzzled.

"What on earth were you doing fighting over the baby Jesus?" John asked Rock.

He looked off to the side. "I wanted to get it back for her." He nodded toward Gran.

"How'd you know where to find it?"

"Because I'm the one who took it, okay? Took it, and threw it in a dumpster. And I had to get it back, that's all. Wasn't gonna let no one take it away from me, either." He glared at the desk officer, whom, Annie now realized, was sporting quite a shiner himself.

"Do you still have it, young man?" Gran asked the officer.

"I do, and it's being held as evidence."

"May I see it, please?" Gran's eyes were sparkling with expectation.

No one could refuse Gran anything when she turned on the charm; Annie knew that from experience. The officer grunted and went back around the corner to another office. Thirty seconds later, he emerged with the baby Jesus doll.

"That's my baby Jesus!" Gran said. "May I have it, please?"

"Is it stolen property?"

Gran looked evenly at Rock. "You were just borrowing it, weren't you, young man?"

"I..."

"Of course you were." She held out her hand to the police officer. "I'll thank you to give it back to me immediately. I need to take it home and put it in the manger. You do know the story, don't you?"

"I know it," the officer grouched. "I'll have to talk to the chief. And so will all of you." The officer disappeared again, doll under his arm.

"You fought that cop?" one of the guys whispered to Rock in a low voice. "What are you, nuts? You don't fight a cop."

"They were takin' his Jesus," Boone said, laughing.

John frowned. "This isn't funny, boys. Don't forget, you're all a short trip away from juvie. We don't need police involvement."

"Well, if the property wasn't stolen, he can't be arrested, right?"

"Sure he can. Breaking and entering, evading arrest...they've got the goods on him if they want to use them."

"That's right." The police chief, a tall, muscular man, emerged. "Gentleman. And ladies. Merry Christmas."

"Merry Christmas," they chorused dutifully.

But the sight of this particular officer pushed Annie back into that horrible time fifteen years ago. The police chief had been one of the officers who'd worked on Rhonda's case. Her breath caught as the memories assailed her.

"It would be a lot merrier if you'd let us take Rock home," John said. "I'm his guardian and I can speak to his being well-disciplined there."

"Not so fast." The chief held out a hand. "You're with the Covenant School, correct?"

"Yes."

Annie forced herself to pay attention through the haze of awful memories. This was now, and this was important. She didn't have to sink back into sorrow and depression.

"There have been complaints in the neighborhood about kids vandalizing things and running wild. With this additional charge, I'm afraid we'll have to look carefully at the school's charter. If it's deemed a threat to the community..."

"It's anything but a threat, young man," Grandma said, drawing herself up to her full, five-foot-two height and putting one hand on her hip. "Why, I'd call it an asset to the community. Those boys are out shoveling and clearing walks and mowing all the time.

They're hard workers. They've renovated the academy and the house beside it. They're wonderful neighbors. There may be other problem teenagers in the area, but these boys are good citizens."

John was studying Annie, and she could read the question in his eyes—was it she who'd called in a complaint about the school?

Thinking about Rhonda, a tear escaped, but she had to let the past go. Let it *go.* Now, these boys and this school were the important thing. "Look," she said, "I was initially worried about the kids, but they haven't been a problem. And I don't think they will be in the future. Can't you let us take them home, Chief?"

He was studying her. "Hey, I know you. You look like..."

She nodded steadily. "You helped investigate my sister's murder about fifteen years ago."

The room went silent as everyone—the boys, John, and Gran—digested what had just been said. Annie moved closer to Gran and put an arm around her.

The police chief shook his head. "That

was one of the worst cases I ever saw. I'll never forget it."

Annie swallowed. "I won't either, but we're here now, and I believe the school's good and that this young man—" she put a hand on Rock's shoulder "—is an asset to the neighborhood. Can't you let him come home on Christmas?"

He studied her. "If you're willing to trust him, given all you've been through, I can't do any less."

Annie blinked. *She* was a model for trusting a teenager? That had to be a Christmas miracle.

"I guess I can treat this as a runaway situation," he said, frowning, "since it's Christmas. But we're going to be keeping a close eye on the school and the boys in it."

"Thank you!" John shook the man's hand, and after glaring at all the boys, they did the same.

"I'm sorry to cause trouble, sir," Rock said of his own volition.

Out in the parking lot, they hugged and fist-bumped each other.

"Come on," Daniel said with the resilience of youth, "We gotta get our tattoos!"

"Hang on," Rock said. He took the bag that held the doll and handed it to Gran. "I'm sorry I took it. And I... Thanks for what you did in there."

Gran's face was radiant. "What's Christmas about but getting the Christ child back, every single year?"

10

The next few hours were a whirl of cooking and Christmas music and relief. Gran had thought to put the turkey in the oven during breakfast, and now they all pitched in to mash potatoes and chop celery to jazz up their stuffing from a box.

Around the dinner table, the boys were loud and raucous, telling stories of their times before they'd come to the school, explaining to Gran and Annie what had gotten them into trouble. "But it's different now," Zeke explained, giving the rest of the boys an older brother glare. "We've got the bond, or we're gonna." He nodded toward the book of tattoos.

"The bond's why I had to go get Jesus back," Rock said around a mouthful of stuffing. "I couldn't make the promise with that on my conscience."

"Then it's already doing some good," John said. "But remember, it's you boys who have to enforce it within yourselves. Like Rock did."

"And if we screw up, we're gonna hunt each other down," Boone said.

"Keep tabs on each other all our lives."

Annie looked at John over the candles that lit the table. What a difference he'd made in the lives of these boys.

She let her admiration shine out of her eyes.

He looked away. "We'd better get this stuff cleaned up. Randy's coming in half an hour."

When Annie offered to help, John waved her away. "We'll get it."

"I'm wanting to get back home," Gran said. "I'll pack my things. You stay here if you want, dearie."

Annie watched the boys and John bustle around cleaning up in a well-oiled routine that didn't leave any space for her. "I guess I'll head out," she said when she could get John's attention. "Thanks you so much for having us."

"Thanks for everything," he said, giving her a sidearm hug. Then one of the boys called him and he turned away.

~

GRAN PUTTERED around the house and Annie sat in the living room and twiddled her thumbs. She turned the TV off and on. She tried to read the paper, then a book. Finally, she stood up and started pacing.

"You seem upset, dear," Gran said. "What's eating you?"

Annie flopped down in a chair. "I thought John liked me, but he's all of a sudden acting like he barely knows me."

"How do you feel about him?"

Annie thought of their kiss and smiled. "I really like him. He's amazing."

"Then act on that," Gran urged. "He's a nice man, a good man."

"But you know I haven't been serious about anyone, ever."

"Because you let what happened to Rhonda ruin your life. You know, though, the Lord makes all things new. He can clean your heart, help you love again."

"But if I hadn't gotten involved with Terrance, maybe Rhonda wouldn't have met up with the group home residents at all." There it was, her own guilt, the reason John's position echoed in her mind, the reason she hadn't wanted to get involved with him. "I feel guilty about loving when Rhonda can't."

"Rhonda is enjoying more love than we can even imagine," Gran said. "Don't you worry about her. She's in the hands of the Lord."

"Do you really believe that?"

"I know it for sure. Rhonda was an innocent, one of the world's most loving people. God didn't turn his back on her. She suffered, yes, and that was terrible. But now she's with him in glory."

"I wish I could feel as sure as you do."

"Just start with what faith you have, dear. If you have the tiniest mustard seed of faith, the Lord can take it and build it. And wouldn't you rather live a life full of faith, and love, than a life like your mother's, full of fear?"

"I...I would. I really would."

Gran sat down beside her. "Then give him your heart. For real. All of it. And see where he leads you."

Annie looked into Gran's eyes. "I don't have much faith, but I have a little seed of it. And I want peace. Joy. What you have."

"Then ask him to help you. Pray every day, and read your Bible, and he'll rebuild your life."

"Really?"

"If you believe." Gran reached across Annie to the end table and handed her a New Testament. "That's a promise. And this book, here, is full of them. That's what Christmas is all about."

~

THE SUN WAS SINKING low in the west by the time the boys were done with their tattoos. John had stuck around for all of it but declined to get a tattoo himself. The Sacred Bond brotherhood wasn't about him, it was about these boys and their potential in the world. He'd told them as much, had hung out with them watching bad TV and eating leftovers and sympathizing about their sore, newly tattooed arms.

"Look, take a break," Zeke had told him finally. "Go over and see Annie. You know you want to."

"Yeah," Rock said. "You're driving us nuts. Get outta here."

"We're fine, John. Go see your lady."

"Book it."

It was true, he wanted to get outside. Felt an urge to get out of the house.

The boys had their whole lives in front of them. He was so proud of them and he eagerly expected them to do well in the world. And to do good. He was proud of himself, too, for the role he'd played.

The Covenant School was doing what it was supposed to do. A lifetime dream was coming true. And he'd stay and keep working on it, with new generations of boys. He was truly satisfied in his work, and for that, he thanked God.

But look at him, living here in an apartment at a school, all alone. On Christmas, all his friends were with their families, and though he'd had invitations, he didn't want to intrude. So here he was, alone.

He knew why, too. Deep inside, he was still waiting for Emily, his first love, still hoping she'd come back to him.

But Emily had moved on long ago. She was married to someone else, and it was wrong of him to hold onto that hope.

He had to let it go. With God's help, he had to let *her* go. And as he thought it, as he prayed it, he opened the school's front door and blinked in the brilliant sparkle of sunshine on snow.

A vise he'd kept tight around his heart all of these years seemed to let loose.

It is not good for a man to be alone.

"You said it, God," he muttered, "way back in the Garden of Eden." He was outside now, and the late afternoon sky glowed pink and violet above the houses and buildings. He didn't know what he was looking for out here; he just knew the walls were confining him.

"Out for a walk?"

The voice, Annie's, told him exactly what

he was looking for and why he'd headed this way. "Yeah. You too?"

She nodded. "I...actually, I was hoping I'd see you."

John's heart gave a little leap. "I'm glad to see you too." But as she fell into step with him, he reminded himself that she lived in Florida and had a great job there. What could he offer her but a place in a rundown neighborhood, *and* a bunch of delinquent boys she didn't like? And yeah, maybe she'd warmed up to the four that were here, but there would always be more. He couldn't even blame her for her attitude, after what had happened to her twin sister. Who was he to counter all that trauma?

"I guess you'll be going home soon," he said.

"My flight back is tomorrow."

He nodded, and the joy he'd felt when he'd seen her slipped away.

"But John," she said, squaring her shoulders like it was costing her to say this, "I don't want to go. I...I'm getting to like it here."

"Really? You like the cold?"

"If you're with the right people, it's not cold, it's warm."

His breath caught and he felt like he couldn't believe his ears. Was she saying what he hoped she was saying?

"It's seemed a lot warmer to me," he said, "since you got here." They'd circled the block and they were back in front of her house now, and she was going to pull away and go in if he didn't speak up now. "Listen," he said, "I want you to come up here."

He tugged her through the snowdrifts and they landed, laughing, in front of the nativity scene. There was the baby, wrapped and out in the manger. "Miss Clara didn't want to keep it inside, to make sure it stays safe?"

She shook her head. "My gran has a lot of faith. In God and in people." She paused, then added, "I'm trying to learn from her."

"Do you want to stick around," he asked, gathering all his courage, "stick around here and see if we can make a go of things?"

"What do you mean, make a go of things?"

"Annie," he said. "We haven't known each other long, but I already know that what I feel for you is different from anything I've ever felt before. I respect and admire you so much, and I like talking to you. And I especially like kissing you." He moved closer and gave her a quick but thorough kiss. No sense not pressing his advantage. "I want to date you and romance you and if all goes well," he swallowed, "and if you agree, we can get married someday."

Her eyes were wide and a little scared. "I'm not that good at relationships, and I'm not good with kids," she said.

"You sure about that? The boys pretty much pushed me out the door to come over here. They seem to like you."

"I like them too," she said. "Oh, John, I can't make any promises, and I can't move fast, but you're the first man who's made it seem worthwhile to try." She paused and added, "I have some growing to do in the faith. I warn you, it's not going to be all quick and easy."

"If there's one thing being older has taught me," he said, "it's that quick and easy is overrated." And then he kissed her, long and slow this time.

EPILOGUE

One Year Later...

ANNIE LOOKED FONDLY at the three boys who stood on the steps of the Covenant School with her and John. "Where's Zeke?" she asked.

"It's freezing out here," Daniel complained.

"This sports coat's definitely cramping my style." Rock shrugged his linebacker shoulders uncomfortably.

A car pulled up and parked down the street, and Boone headed toward it. "That's him!"

She smiled up at John. "I just really want a picture in front of the school. Thanks for humoring me."

"It's my pleasure." He looked stunning in a dark suit, a red flower in his lapel. His arm came around her easily and he pulled her close for a quick kiss.

"I'm here, I'm here." Zeke arrived in a business suit. He had scored a job during the winter break, managing a local department store.

Annie looked down at her white velvet wedding dress. She felt like a queen. And John made her feel more like that every day.

Even more, she knew who she was in Christ. A new creation, born in love.

She was running a PR campaign for the school, trying to improve its image, and recently two other nonprofits had contracted for her services. She could work out of her home office, here in the remodeled house where Gran still lived.

"Wait for me!" Gran emerged from the

school where she'd been staying warm, wearing a long mink coat that made her look like an old-time movie star. .An adjustment in her medications had been all it took to make her minor memory problems go away. At ninety, she was doing great, even volunteering here at the school.

This year, there was a new generation of boys who needed help. There was so much to do.

"Hang on," Boone said, and ducked back into the building. A minute later he emerged with Macy, who'd become the school's unofficial mascot. "Can't have a group picture without the dog."

Whiskers sat with dignity on the inside windowsill. No way was she coming outside.

As the photographer snapped away, Annie lifted her face to the sunshine, feeling its warmth. She was looking forward to the future. Not focused inward, on her own pain anymore, but outward, on how she could serve and help others.

The man who would become her husband in less than an hour pulled her into his arms. "This is the best day of my life," he said.

"Me too." She looked up at him, then leaned her head on his shoulder. "At least, the best day so far."

SACRED BOND SERIES

Have you read the other Sacred Bond novels?

A Christmas Bond (Christian Romance): Sacred Bond Series Prequel Novella

War hero John Moretti must work with crime victim Annie Bauer to restore the Baby Jesus to Annie's grandmother's yard nativity scene... or risk sending the boys he mentors straight to juvie.

His Baby Bond (Christian Romance): Sacred Bond Series Book 1

On a Colorado mountaintop, poor-but-proud Kendra Forrester battles millionaire

Zeke King for custody of the baby they both love…

The Bride's Broken Bond (Christian Romance): Sacred Bond Series Book 2

Poor little rich girl Hope DeMille runs away from her high-society wedding, straight into the inner city…and into the brawny arms of urban missionary Rock Anderson.

Her Reunion Bond (Christian Romance): Sacred Bond Series Book 3

What if your high school boyfriend came back to town…and moved in next door?

The Doctor's Bond (Christian Romance): Sacred Bond Series Book 4

The bad boy from the wrong side of the tracks is now a respected doctor…but he's still a little too edgy for the proper preacher's daughter. Or is he?

ABOUT THE AUTHOR

Lee Tobin McClain is the New York Times bestselling author of more than forty novels. A professor-turned-writer, she finds inspiration in her beautiful and brilliant daughter, her goofy goldendoodle, and her aptly named cat, Trouble.

Connect with Lee and join her newsletter:
www.leetobinmcclain.com

COPYRIGHT PAGE

Lee Tobin McClain: McClain@setonhill.edu
www.leetobinmcclain.com

Printed in Dunstable, United Kingdom

75909632R00221